Winter Hill Farm

by New York Times Bestselling Author

JOE HILLEY

Dunlavy + Gray
HOUSTON

WINTER HILL FARM

Dunlavy + Gray ©2023 by Joe Hilley

Library of Congress Control Number: 2023949123

ISBN: 979-8-9868156-4-0

E-Book ISBN: 979-8-9868156-5-7

This book is a work of fiction. Names, characters, businesses, organizations, places, events, and incidents either are the product of the author's imagination or are used fictitiously. Any resemblance to any person, living or dead, is coincidental.

Cover design and typesetting by Fitz & Hill Creative Studio.

First Printing, 2023
Printed in the United States of America

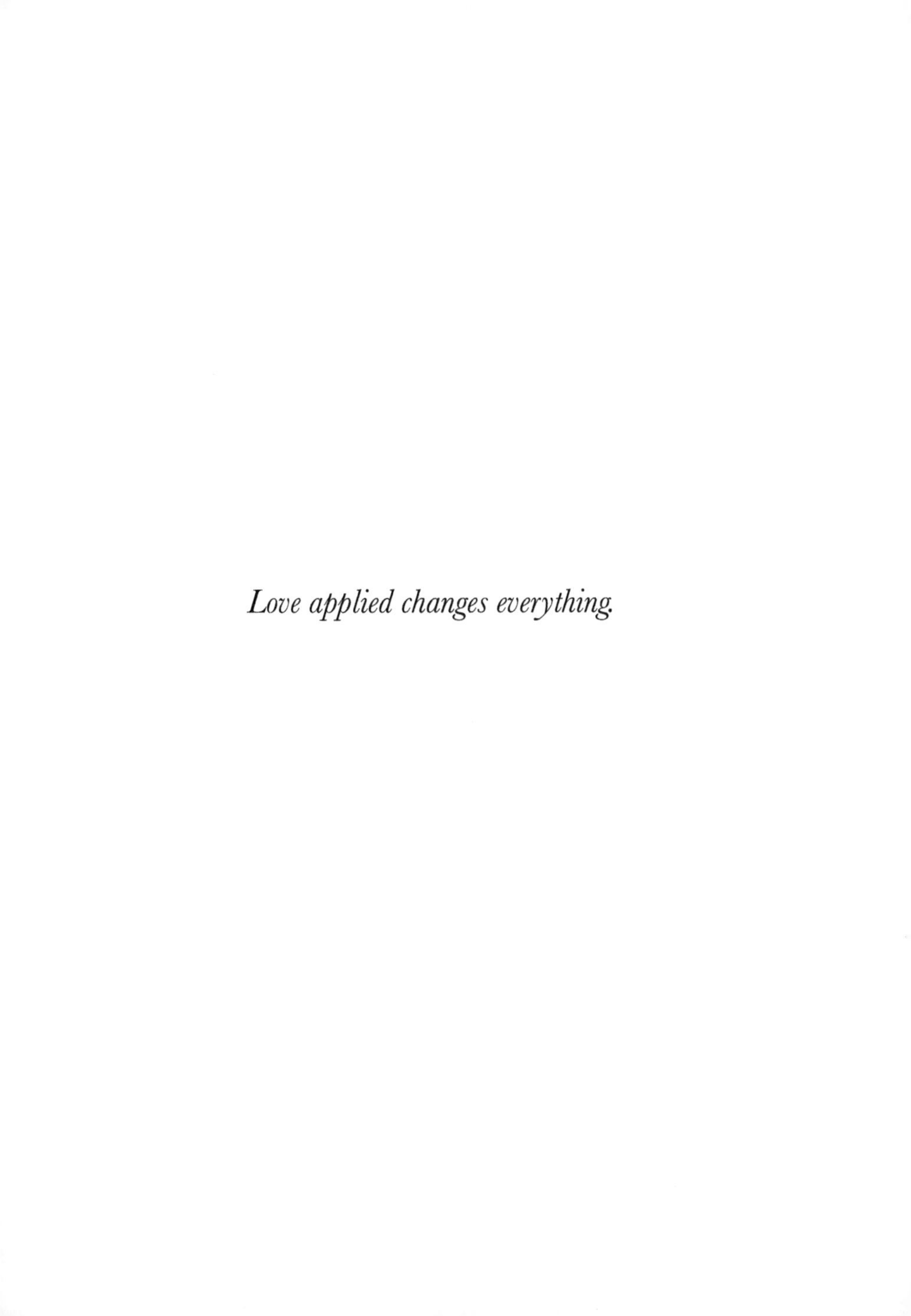

Love applied changes everything.

CHAPTER 1

It was one of those Saturday mornings you remember long after the day has passed. Not the date or the time, not even the year, but the look and the feel of it. Brilliant sunshine. A sky so incredibly blue it defies description. The kind of day that brings with it the certainty, merely from seeing it through the window, that the air outside is crisp and thin and light. "A chamber of commerce day," my uncle used to say. "The reason people come to the coast in winter." The Gulf Coast. The northern part, to be exact. A thousand miles of meandering shoreline stretching from Apalachicola, Florida, to Brownsville, Texas.

From the window at my desk, I had a commanding view of the day and all its glory. Mid-term exams were approaching, and I had been trying to prepare for them, but the sky was so beautiful, the sun so bright. And from the cool air that seeped through the cracks in the window frame, I knew it was a day too wonderful to spend inside on books and study and lessons. It was a day for a walk. An aimless stroll. Maybe I could find Sterling, my roommate, and convince him to join me. A leisurely walk then lunch, perhaps. I checked my watch. It was not quite ten, a little early for eating. Coffee, then. Sterling liked coffee and there was a shop not far from campus.

Before I could move from the desk, a shout came from the hall. "Hey, Jake. There's a girl on the phone for you." A girl. Calling on Saturday. There was only one girl who would do that. Julia. My heart skipped a beat at the thought of her.

I turned away from the window, pushed myself up from the chair, and started toward the pay phone that hung on the wall in the stairwell. Payphone. A shout from the hall. Dorm life. The year was 1971.

When I reached the phone, I found the receiver dangling by the cord. I took it in my left hand and placed one end against my ear, the other was near my lips. Before I could speak, I heard Julia's voice. "Jake," she began. I knew from the way she said my name there was trouble. Her voice always gave her away when she was scared and right then I knew something was wrong. Someone was sick. Or someone had died. Or something equally terrible had happened.

"What's the matter?" I asked.

"Jake," she sobbed. "I'm pregnant."

Today, that might not sound like much. Women get pregnant all the time, and many aren't married when they do. No one seems to care now. But back then, getting pregnant without being married was a big deal. Abortion wasn't an option. Not for Julia. Not for me. Not for anyone. Certainly, not for anyone we knew.

My heart sank and I stared at the wall, unable to speak, feeling the world collapse around me. A future, carefully mapped and planned, evaporated in an instant. Hopes and dreams that reached the core of my being shriveled up and disappeared in an undoing for whom I could blame no one but myself.

When I didn't respond immediately, Julia's voice changed from worried to desperate. "Jake? Are you there, Jake?"

I moved the receiver closer to my mouth and cleared my throat. "Yeah," I said slowly. "I'm here."

"What are we going to do?"

With all my heart, I wanted to say something that would make the whole thing right. Put it all back in its place. As if it had been only a few minutes earlier when I was staring out the window and thinking how wonderful the day was. To rewind time to a moment before the phone rang, when Julia and I could dream and laugh and play without the guilt that now seeped into every corner of our being. But I didn't know what to say. So, I asked, "Got any ideas for a name?"

Julia started crying. "How can you make a joke at a time like this?"

"I wasn't joking," I replied, and I wasn't joking, but that didn't seem to matter. She cried all the more and I felt awful. "Listen, we'll work this out," I said. It was the kind of lame response people give when they face a confounding situation, but it also was the truth. We would work it out. We had no other choice.

"But how?" she asked.

How—that was the question. The big question. The real question. Bigger and more real than anyone could know. The answer to it would turn both our lives in the opposite direction we'd been headed just moments before. One minute this, the next minute that. With no time to think, consider, or ponder. "I'll come home," I said, "and we can talk about it then." And there it was, the turning of our lives.

"When?" she asked.

"It's Saturday." I sighed. "No one will be in the office until Monday."

"The office?" She sounded puzzled.

"I'll have to withdraw," I explained. "If I ever want to come back, I can't just leave. I have to withdraw and to do that, I have to talk to someone in the office."

"Oh."

From the tone of her voice, I knew she understood what withdrawing meant. I was a student at Spring Hill College. Gaining admission had been difficult, but there was no point in worrying about that now. I should have thought of it earlier. Before we did what we did to get where we were.

"It'll be all right," I said bravely. "I'll see you on Monday."

By the time the call ended, I was in no mood for coffee with Sterling or anyone else. I wanted to be alone, so I took my jacket from the room and went outside. Walking, however, proved less of a relief than I thought. I hadn't gone a hundred yards before my legs felt tired and heavy. I pressed on, though, forcing my muscles to exert themselves. Pushing back against the weight that seemed to bear upon me. Pushing me downward, toward the gathering darkness in my mind. Toward despair.

We'd had such hopes. Such dreams. Such visions of the future. A life. A career. With endless possibilities. None of that seemed possible now. All of it dashed upon the rocks of a single night. A single instance. A single moment.

In a few minutes, I reached the campus gate at the street. A bench was there, beneath a live oak that covered it with shade, making the air especially cool. I took a seat and for a long time sat staring across the campus to the spire of the chapel, visible through the trees, its sharp angles outlined against the sky. A metaphoric symbol of right and wrong not lost on me, as if I needed another reminder of how gravely I had failed. The sense of judgment, guilt, and shame that came over me as I talked to Julia now sank into my soul with an intensity I could hardly bear.

For certain, I wasn't the first college freshman to father a child with his girlfriend, but right then it felt like it. And I suppose I should have been thinking of Julia and not of myself. After all, I could walk down the street, and no one would know the truth of what I'd done just from looking at me. Julia didn't have that luxury. Wherever she went, people would know from her soon-to-be protruding belly that she was carrying a child. Everyone who knew her would know she wasn't married. They would look at her and without saying a word she would get the message. "I know what you've been doing." And she would feel their condemnation.

That's what Julia was thinking about when she called. I could hear it in her voice when we spoke on the phone. She was ashamed and that was all she had right now. Not hope or anticipation. Not fear of the pain that awaited her in nine months or the dread of dirty diapers and late-night feedings. Not even anxiety about the dreams and plans that now seemed hopeless. All she had was shame. I, however, had only fear, and that fear had a face—my father's.

From the time my father was old enough to talk, his one ambition in life had been to become a New Orleans policeman. His father was a policeman, as was his father before him. Two of my uncles were policemen, as were three cousins. It was in the family blood. The day after his high school graduation, my grandfather—Pop-Pop—drove my father to police headquarters and signed him up for a patrolman's job. Afterward, Pop-Pop introduced him to the chief and said, "This boy's gonna make us proud."

That story was repeated more times than I could remember, and almost every time Dad told it he was cussing me for something I'd done that he didn't like. Before I was six, I knew I would never make him proud, and now I was certain of it. He was a hard man, and impossible to please. Not physically abusive, just unrelenting. And he was always there, patrolling our lives the same way he patrolled the beat. If he'd been absent from the house—drinking all night with his buddies, or fishing on weekends—things wouldn't have been so bad. At least then we would've had a break from him. But he wasn't like that and there was never a reprieve from the constant thud, thud, thud of his footsteps coming to check on me to see what I was doing, then needling me for days about whatever he thought I'd done wrong.

Now I had to tell him Julia was pregnant, and I was the father. I wasn't worried that he would beat me, but I was certain he would respond with that mocking, derisive laugh he always gave when I had done something he didn't like. A laugh and a sneer and a shake of his head that cut me to the bone. Then he would sigh and mutter, "What an idiot," as he slumped back in his chair.

From the moment Julia told me, I knew what to do. I had to go home, tell everyone what happened, and get on with being Julia's husband and the father of the child she was carrying. I was sitting on that bench hoping I could think of something else we could do, but knowing all the while there wasn't anything else that could be done. Only the right thing. The responsible thing. But even doing that wouldn't address the final part of the problem.

When I was twelve, I signed up to be an altar boy at St. Dominic's, our local parish church. That's how I first got the idea of becoming a priest. I was mesmerized by the ritual of

Holy Communion, the way the priest washed his hands in the basin and dried them with the cloth that was draped over my arm. The arrangement of everything on the altar table, placing the paten, cup, and book in just the right position. And when it was ready, the melodic words of the prayers echoing through the sanctuary. Back then, we still did one service in Latin, even though the Pope said we didn't have to, and I used to love hearing the words roll off Father Deasy's tongue. It sounded like music to me.

As one might expect, Dad was adamantly opposed to me being a priest. It was fine to attend church and believe in God and all that. It was great to volunteer and assist in the services. But no one in his family had ever been a minister in any church, of any denomination, and he didn't want it for me. He wanted me to follow in his footsteps and become a cop. "The family business," he called it. But that was his dream, and I wasn't interested in pursuing it. He didn't force me to stop serving in church; he just never encouraged me in it. And he never missed an opportunity to remind me of the things I had to give up as a priest, sex being his primary point. I thought of only the things I would gain.

Then one day at school I noticed Julia. She'd been in our class since third grade, but she was always the skinny girl with braces and clunky glasses who sat in the front row. When we went out to the playground, she kept to herself and spent the time reading a book while the rest of us screamed and yelled and ran around like idiots. But sometime during the summer after our freshman year, that all changed. When school began the next fall, she was a statuesque brunette with long legs, beautiful hips, and breasts that made you look at her even if you tried not to. During the second week of class, I asked her out on a date for a school dance and to my surprise she accepted. After that, we were together every weekend.

Mama liked her and was always glad to have her around. Dad noticed all the things about her that everyone else noticed and chided me constantly with comments like, "Thought you wanted to be a priest, boy. Can't have no girlfriends if you're a priest." If I didn't respond, he kept going, adding graphic descriptions of the sexual things I wouldn't be able to do. Mama usually stopped him when he got to the part about priests and nuns and the children they bore in secret. I would like to say I ignored him, but I didn't, and his comments only heightened my sense of guilt over my feelings toward Julia. I needed someone to talk to, but Dad wasn't the talking kind, other than harassing me, and I couldn't tell Mama. So, with no one else to rely on, I turned to Father Deasy.

One Saturday morning, as we were leaving the sacristy after early Mass, I asked if we could talk. He pointed to a pew, and we took a seat. Then he looked over at me. "What's on your mind?"

"I was wondering if priests ever missed living a regular life." I was unsure how to begin and the beginning I chose sounded awful, but I stuck with it and waited for him to respond.

He looked puzzled. "Regular life?"

"You know, parties, friends, girls."

"Ahh," he nodded and smiled as if suddenly understanding where this was going. "I attend parties, and I have many friends." He looked over at me again. "Are you still considering the priesthood?"

"Yes," I said slowly. "But how do you do it?"

"Do what? Become a priest? We've talked about that before. You have to—"

"The girls," I said, cutting him off. "How do you handle the girls?"

"Oh." He smiled. "Well—"

"It's not like that," I added, trying to head him off before he asked too many questions. "It's just—"

"You know," he began before I finished, "just because you said the priesthood was your intention when you were twelve, doesn't mean you have to follow that path now." I was impressed that he remembered how old I was when we had our first conversation on the topic. And I guess I should have taken the bait right then, thrown over the whole idea of being a priest, and planned my life in a different direction. But it seemed like I would be giving up on something just because doing it proved difficult and I didn't like giving up. "I know," I replied. "But that's not it. I'm just wondering how to get past it."

He frowned again. "Past what?"

"The way I feel when I look at her."

He raised an eyebrow. "Her?"

"Julia."

"Well," he said slowly, "I don't think you can ever get past that."

Now it was my turn to frown. "What do you mean?"

"I mean, you're a man, or soon will be, and she's a woman. That's how we're made."

"You mean, the thoughts aren't wrong?"

"I mean," he said, "they're unavoidable. Thoughts, feelings, physical arousal. You'll never get away from it."

The topic made me uncomfortable, but I was intrigued by his answers, so I kept going. "You think those thoughts, too?"

"Not so much anymore," he said with a shrug. "I'm getting a little older now and it's not as much of a problem as it was when I was younger." He chuckled. "But I still notice when a woman walks by."

This was far more honest a discussion than I could have ever imagined. I had expected to hear a sermon on abstinence and the sin of lust. Instead, I found myself sitting on the pew next to a man who talked to me as a man talked with his friends. We could just as easily have been sitting on a tire at Phil's service station.

Then I noticed something else. The guilt I'd been carrying for months was no longer on my back. I felt free and light, but my mind couldn't quite believe what I'd heard was the truth. "I don't understand," I said, shaking my head.

"Priests have those thoughts, and that's okay?"

"The priest's life isn't about becoming immune to the attractions of the opposite sex," he replied. "It's more like a diet. We know those things are delicious and wonderful. We just choose not to make them a part of our lifestyle. At least, most of us do. Some handle it better than others. Whether you become a priest or not, you'll face the same dilemma over many issues, and you will have to choose the things you make part of your life. You'll face that question no matter what vocation you choose."

In a way, I had made a choice when I continued to see Julia after Father Deasy and I talked. We dated through high school and were committed to each other when I left to attend Spring Hill. The choice to be with her became irrevocable when I went back in September and spent a weekend with her at the apartment of a friend in Metairie. Now, I faced another choice. Not about whether to be a priest; that decision was already made. If I attempted to pursue that goal, the bishop would find out I had a child, and he would never let me advance to ordination. The choice I faced now was whether to run and hide and leave Julia to deal with the consequences of what we did or stay and face up to it. I already knew the answer to that question, too.

After a while on the bench by the college entrance, I realized the campus was quiet and still. I glanced around and saw the sun was setting. A check of my watch told me I had been there all afternoon, and it was almost time for dinner.

As I rose from the bench and started back to the dorm, I was resolved to make the only choice that offered any hope for us. First thing Monday morning, I would withdraw from school, go home, and face the situation head-on. But I dreaded the thought of telling my father.

CHAPTER 2

The next day was Sunday. I attended the earliest Mass, then a cousin from Coden picked me up and I disappeared for the day, ambling back to campus shortly before dinnertime. No one seemed to notice my absence, which was fine with me.

When I awoke on Monday morning, Sterling was already up and dressed. "You're gonna miss breakfast," he said. His voice was much too excited for the earliness of the hour.

"Not missing much," I grumbled, and slid deeper beneath the cover.

"Well, you better get moving," he urged. "You don't want to miss Wainwright's class. He's supposed to give us some insight into the midterm exam." Wainwright gave an all-essay test, but he told his students the questions ahead of time, which made the test less of a test and more of a learning event. I enjoyed it and was sad to be leaving it behind.

When I didn't respond, Sterling grabbed my foot and shook it. "Come on," he urged. "Get moving."

The sense of dread about my situation that had hung

over me on Saturday, with only brief relief on Sunday, suddenly returned and fell on me with an oppressive heaviness. Sterling had been my friend for only a few months, but we'd lived together in the dorm room and took most of our classes together. I couldn't leave without telling him why.

"I'm not going to class," I replied quietly.

"Yeah," he scoffed. "Like that would ever happen. Come on." He slapped my leg. "Get moving."

I threw aside the covers, swung my feet to the floor, and sat on the edge of the bed. "Seriously," I insisted as I rubbed my hands over my face. "I'm not going to class."

He glanced down at me, his forehead wrinkled in a look of concern. "Why not?"

"I'll…tell you later." Suddenly I wasn't sure I should tell him at all, but we had become close, and I needed his help getting to the bus station. "After class," I said. "I'll tell you after class."

"No," Sterling replied. The look in his eyes was intense, and they were focused on me. "You'll tell me now," he insisted. "What's this about?"

I ignored his question and slipped on my pants. "Has your car got any gas in it?"

"Yes," he said. "Why?"

"Come back after class. I'll be waiting for you."

He was standing near his desk. "You're scaring me, Jake."

"Don't be afraid." I glanced at the clock on the shelf by the bed. "But you better hurry. The bell's about to ring."

He checked his watch, then grabbed his books and turned toward the door. "We're not finished with this."

"Just come back after class," I replied.

By then, he was out the door. I paused, one leg in the trouser, the other not, and waited to hear him call in response, but all I heard was the pounding of his feet echoing through the stairwell as he went down to the first floor.

After Sterling was gone, I got dressed and walked over to the registrar's office. The lady who worked at the front counter sat at a desk a few feet behind it. She peered at me over her dark-rimmed glasses as if I was interrupting her well-planned morning. When I told her I wanted to withdraw, she rose from her chair and came to where I stood. She paused there across from me with her fingers laced together on the countertop, her head cocked at an imperious angle. "And just why would you want to do such a thing as that?"

"I have some personal business I have to take care of," I answered, avoiding her piercing glare. "I need to go home."

The corners of her mouth turned up in a disapproving frown, but I ignored her and waited while she took a form from beneath the counter. She slapped it on the countertop and handed me a pen. "Fill it out," she said tersely. "Make sure you include an address where we can reach you."

Fifteen minutes later, I was back at the dorm, packing. When Sterling returned from class, I was finished and seated at my desk.

"Wainwright's looking for you," he said as he burst into the room.

"What for?"

"He wants to see you."

"What did he say?"

"When I told him you weren't coming to class, he looked angry," Sterling said. He took a seat on my bed. "Now tell me what's going on. What was it you wouldn't tell me earlier?"

"I'm going home," I replied.

"What for? It's Monday."

"I'm not going for a visit," I explained. "I withdrew from school."

Sterling had a horrified look. "Withdrew?" he exclaimed. "You're quitting?"

"Yeah."

"But why?"

"There's stuff I have to——"

Just then, the door flew open again and Wainwright entered the room. He was younger than most of the faculty, with thick curly hair and a narrow chin that gave him a boyish look, which the girls in our class found irresistible. He was everyone's favorite and intellectually superior to anyone we'd ever known.

As he came through the doorway, his cheeks were rosy, and he was out of breath from running up the stairs. "The registrar called me," he blurted out. "You can't leave. Not now. You're just getting started."

"Why did the registrar call you?"

"I'm your academic adviser," he said. "Now, what's this about?"

"I have to go," I replied calmly. "I have no choice."

Wainwright pushed the door closed and moved farther into the room. "Why? Why do you have to leave now?"

"We were just about to get to that," Sterling said.

I looked up at Wainwright. "Julia is pregnant," I said flatly.

Wainwright's shoulders sagged. "Damn," he whispered, and he sat down hard on the bed next to Sterling. "When did that happen?"

"I went home for a weekend."

"Hmm," he groaned, shaking his head. "How far along is she?"

"About two months."

"Two months." He frowned, as if calculating in his mind. "That would have been about the time you arrived."

"I went home the first weekend."

Wainwright flopped backward on the bed. "You had so much potential." Almost as soon as the words were out of his mouth, he sat up straight and looked me in the eye. "You still have potential," he said, pointing his finger at me. "This is not over. You cannot escape God like this."

I shrugged. "I don't want to escape Him. I just don't have any other choice right now."

"What are you going to do?" he asked. "I mean, how is

this going to work out?"

"I'll get a job. Marry Julia. Raise our child."

Wainwright smiled. "The responsible thing."

"I guess so," I shrugged again.

"Any parent would be proud of you for that decision." He stood and placed his hand on my shoulder. "They won't say so now," he added. "When you tell them about this, they'll only think of the act that caused the problem. But later, when they've had time to think about it and see how much you've done, they'll be proud of how you handled it."

I bristled at the way he referred to our child and the creation of it as a problem. What Julia and I did that weekend hadn't felt like a problem. We thought of it as an act of love and intimacy. A moment unlike either of us had ever experienced before. "It wasn't exactly like—"

"Yes," Wainwright said, cutting me off in a professorial tone. "It was a selfish act, and it has created a problem for you. But I know you can't see that now."

If anyone else had said that I might have answered them with a fist, but he wasn't anyone. He was Wainwright. So, I smiled and nodded politely.

"You'll need to tell your father first," he added. "He can get your mother on your side."

Wainwright didn't know my father or the dynamics of our family. And by then I'd had all the sermonizing I could take. But rather than arguing about it, I stood and gripped the handle of my suitcase. "Well," I sighed, "I would love to stay and chat, but I need to get going." I looked over at Sterling. "Can you give me a ride to the bus station?"

"Sure," he replied. He opened the door and waited while Wainwright stepped out to the hallway. I followed and Sterling closed the door after us, then we trooped downstairs together.

Wainwright and I said our final goodbye on the sidewalk. He seemed genuinely sad to see me go, and I was sorry to leave, but the decision was made, and I had to get home. We shook hands and slapped each other on the back, then Sterling and I started toward the car.

When we were out of earshot, Sterling leaned near me. "Sorry about that. I didn't know he would show up at the dorm and give you a lecture."

"It's okay," I replied. "I think he meant well."

"I'm sure he did, but sometimes he doesn't seem to realize there are boundaries to his relationship with us."

"Boundaries," I chuckled.

Sterling looked offended. "What's so funny about that?"

"I don't know," I replied. "It just sounds funny coming from you. And in the present context."

"Yeah," he grinned. "I guess it does."

Sterling dropped me at the Greyhound bus station on Government Street and I went inside to check the schedule. The next bus to New Orleans left in an hour. I bought a ticket and walked over to the pay phone to call Julia. Our conversation was brief, she was at her parents' house, and it was awkward for her to talk. I gave her the time when the bus would arrive, then took a seat and waited.

Telling my father that Julia was pregnant still worried me, but as I sat there staring at the mural that lined the wall on the opposite side of the room, that worry receded. Instead of focusing on him, I thought of Julia and the baby she was carrying. An odd sense of pride rose inside me, and for the first time, I felt like a father. A man, taking on the responsibilities of life. And it felt good.

Julia was waiting for me when I arrived at the bus station in New Orleans. She seemed relieved to see me and I wondered if she had been worried that I might not show, but I didn't ask. We both were under enough stress as it was. No need to pick a fight over something that didn't matter. I took her hand as we walked through the station and smiled at her when she glanced at me, doing my best to let her think I was glad to be there. Inside, though, the reality of what we faced seemed more real than I could handle. I felt hollow and empty and completely at a loss about what to do next.

When my luggage was loaded in the car and we were beside each other on the front seat, I suggested we have coffee and talk before meeting anyone. She drove us to Café Du Monde on Decatur Street, and we sat at a table.

"Have you told your parents?" I asked.

"No," she said. "But I think my mother suspects some-thing."

"Why?"

"I noticed her looking at me the other day when she was in my room. Women her age say they can tell when a woman's pregnant by the way she looks, long before a man notices." She paused to take a sip of coffee, then added. "I think she's figured it out."

I could tell it, too. A glow. A radiance. Something about her indicated a change from how she used to be. I saw it as I came into the lobby at the station, but I kept it to myself then, and I kept it to myself later when we were having coffee. "Maybe she was thinking about something else," I suggested.

Julia shook her head. "I don't think so."

After we finished our coffee, we drove to Julia's house. Her mother was there alone; it wasn't quite five. She seemed surprised to see me but didn't press the point about me being there at the beginning of the week. When Julia's father arrived from work, we told them the news—Julia was preg-nant, and I dropped out of school to get a job and support her. I assumed we would marry, though Julia and I hadn't discussed it explicitly. He wasn't happy about it, but he didn't hit me, so I counted that part a win. Julia's mother stared at me with a cold, hard look but said nothing.

After dinner, Julia drove us to my parents' house. Dad was in the living room, sitting in the recliner, watching televi-sion. Mom followed us in there. And we told them.

Dad stared at me for a moment, then burst out laughing. "You stupid idiot. Don't you know what a rubber's for?"

Julia was holding my arm, and I felt her cringe when he said it. Anger flew over me and I wanted to hit him, but I held it in and said, "We plan to get married. I'll get a job. We'll get an apartment."

Mom was crying. Dad shook his head. "Good luck with that."

"What do you mean?"

"You don't have any skills," he said. "Best you can do is work as a laborer for somebody, but you never liked working. So, I figure this will all blow over in a month or two."

"Do you think I could be a cop?" It was an emotionally risky question, especially given his initial reaction to us, but being a cop seemed like my best option and a word from him could make it happen.

"Ha!" he cackled. "You can't bang your girlfriend without getting caught. I doubt you'd make much of anything."

"You could put a word in for me," I said.

"I could." He leaned forward, closed the recliner, and stood. "But I ain't."

"Why not?"

Mom spoke up. "Because then he'd have to explain why you weren't in school." She wiped her nose with a tissue. "And that wouldn't look good for him. Or us."

And there it was. The thing that had bugged me all my life. Really bugged me. Deep down. Beneath all the other things he said and did that irritated me. No matter what happened, Dad always had to come out looking good. Not objectively good. Not like, 'My kid is in a jam and I'm helping him out and if you don't like it, you can kiss my ass.' No. That wasn't his idea of looking good. The appearance that mattered to him was having everyone and everything in its place. Neat, orderly, and causing him no grief of any kind whatsoever. By that measure, I had failed miserably all my life.

Rather than endure more of their derisive comments, Julia and I went for a walk. She was crying and I pulled her close. "It'll be okay," I said.

She hit me in the stomach with the back of her hand. "Don't say that. It's not okay."

"We'll make it work," I said. Then I remembered that I had never asked her to marry me. We hadn't even discussed it. I just assumed that's what we would do. So, I reminded her of that and asked, "Is that what you want?"

"What?"

"To get married."

"Yes," she said. "What else would I want?"

"I don't know. I was just thinking we hadn't talked about it between us. You and me. And I wanted to make sure."

"I can't do this by myself."

"Good," I said.

"Good?" She stopped and looked up at me. "Good? You think this is good?"

"Yes," I replied. "We have a child on the way. Father Deasy says children are a blessing. That means we are blessed."

"We can be blessed even if we did it like this?"

"Mary wasn't married when she got pregnant with Jesus."

"That was a different situation."

"Not to her neighbors," I said. "Or to her family."

"It was Jesus she was carrying."

"They didn't know that. And even if they did, can you imagine Mary telling her friends, 'I'm pregnant but it's okay because the Holy Spirit overshadowed me and gave me this baby.' They'd be like, 'That girl has lost her mind.'"

"Well," Julia said. "When you put it like that." And for the first time that day, she smiled.

CHAPTER 3

During those first few weeks, Julia stayed with her parents, and I stayed with mine. I think Dad wanted to throw me out, but for once, Mom stood up for me and wouldn't let him. I heard them arguing about it several times. But they were adamantly against helping in any other way and wouldn't even let me use the car that I'd driven in high school. "It's our car," they said. "And we can't condone what you've done."

After a day or two of that, I said, "What would you rather I did? Ignore Julia? Ignore the baby she's carrying? Find some backstreet butcher to take care of it for her?"

My father stepped closer and leaned toward me, his nose near mine. "You should have prevented it from happening in the first place." He tapped me on the chest with his index finger as he spoke. I hated it when he did that.

I caught Mom's eye. "This is crazy."

"No," she said. "What you did was crazy."

"I can't go back and undo what's already done," I retorted.

"You could let her deal with it," Dad said. "She's the one who's pregnant." The comment was so ludicrous I didn't know what to say, so I kept quiet.

Ignoring them allowed me to stay at their house without getting into a physical altercation, but ignoring our situation wasn't an option for me. Or for Julia. The baby was coming. We had less than nine months to prepare for him or her or all or both. "Please, Lord," I prayed every night. "Let your will be done, but I hope we don't have twins." It was an awful prayer. I should have been giving thanks in every respect, but I felt like there was only me and Julia and a mountain of trouble sliding in our direction.

The first task was to find a job but being forced to rely on public transportation, at least in the meantime, my search for work was confined to areas of the city that were served by the city bus system. Julia had a car, but she was working at a department store downtown and needed her car for that. The sugar plant in Chalmette was one of the city's biggest employers but it was farther away than I wanted, and the city bus only went as far as Arabi. Still, I had to begin some-where, so I began with them. Julia dropped me off at the plant gate in the morning on her way to work.

A lady in the office told me to fill out an application and handed me a blank form. When I completed it, she directed me to another office where I was interviewed by a man who was about my father's age. Clean shaven. Neat haircut slicked back with hair oil. A gray suit that was a little too big, like he bought it off the rack and wore it without having it tailored. He seemed interested in hiring me but didn't make an offer.

The next day, I went to the coffee plant on Old Gentilly Road. It was a long way out, too—farther east than the sugar plant—but I knew a guy who worked there and was pretty sure he would let me ride with him if I got a job there and if we could get on the same shift. Someone at the plant interviewed me and gave me a tour, then said they'd be in touch. I assumed I would never hear from them again, but the next day I received a phone call telling me I'd been hired for their maintenance crew. The day after that, I went to work.

The head of our crew was a man named Bobby Reeves. He was younger than my father but still old enough to be my dad. I enjoyed working with my hands and did my best to fit in. At first, Bobby wasn't sure I was right for the job but then he found out I could remember things in great detail. If we took something apart, I remembered how to put it back together. He liked that because although he was trained to work on most of the equipment, there were some parts he'd never touched. Having a member of his crew who recalled the order in which something had been disassembled was a great asset to him. On our crew, that person was me.

A month after I started at the plant, I found an apartment. Part of an old house that had been divided into separate units. It was about halfway between my parent's house and the coffee plant, and although it was small—one bedroom, one bathroom, and a kitchen that was also the dining room and living room—Julia said we could make it work. Not long after we leased it, I bought a car. It needed some work, but it ran and there wasn't anything wrong with it that I couldn't fix with Bobby's help.

We didn't have any furniture that was ours to take, but friends from high school and acquaintances from work had several pieces they were glad to get rid of. A wardrobe that was missing the mirror. A dresser with a broken drawer. A wobbly dining table. A chair with no cushions. The kind of furniture that people kept in their garage, thinking they would repair it but never did. I repaired and refinished it, then bought a worn-out bedframe and a used mattress from a store down the street. The only thing missing was a refrigerator. We didn't have enough money for one so I bought an ice chest from a boating store, filled it with ice, and set it on the counter near the sink so we could keep the water drained from it. Julia cried when she saw it.

"Is that the best we can do?" she asked.

"It's only for right now," I replied. "We'll find a refrigerator soon."

"But how will we pay for it?"

That was the problem. We had to pay a deposit to get the apartment, which took most of our money, so things were tight financially. "It'll be better in a few weeks," I said. "I'll get paid again."

"But we have to eat," she said. "And the baby will be

here. And we'll need diapers and clothes and bottles and——"

"It's okay." I put my arms around her and held her close. "It'll all work out."

"But how?"

"I don't know. But we don't have to know."

"What do you mean?"

"We only have to know the next thing."

"And what is that?" she asked. "What's the next thing for us?"

"To get married," I replied.

She smiled and wiped her eyes. "Have you told Father Deasy?"

"No. Have you?"

She shook her head. "I thought you'd want to be the one."

My regular shift at the plant ran from eight in the morning until five in the afternoon, Monday through Friday, which gave me Saturdays and Sundays off. Despite that, I had been so busy setting up the apartment and getting used to the job that I had failed to attend Mass three weeks in a row. That was a lot of misses for me. I couldn't remember ever missing Mass at all, much less three weeks' worth. So, the next Saturday after I bought the ice chest, I went to confession at St. Dominic's. Father Deasy was in the booth, and I knew from the sound of his voice that he was glad to have me there. We hadn't talked since I returned from school.

"I understand your situation has changed," he said.

"I suppose word gets around."

"News like that is difficult to contain."

"Then you know some of what I have to confess."

"Let me hear the rest," he said.

Almost a month had gone by since my last confession. Recalling everything that had occurred during that time took a few minutes. When I finished, Father Deasy said, "How do you intend to address the situation with Julia?"

"We want to get married."

"I assume you mean in the church."

"Yes," I replied. "Of course." As a practicing Catholic, there was no other option.

"Before we can do that, I'll need to meet with both of you," he said. "For counseling."

"Okay," I responded. "But we don't have a lot of time before the baby is due." From my experience in the church, I knew he preferred several sessions with a couple before the wedding.

"We'll keep it to the essentials," he said.

Every Saturday after that, Julia and I met with Father Deasy and discussed marriage, how we felt about the pregnancy, the child we would soon have, and the expectations we had for our respective roles. I hadn't thought about it that way—the roles we would play and the mechanics of how marriage might function from a practical perspective. I'd just been moving along from one thing to the next and daydreaming about the guilt-free sex we would have after the baby was born.

Two months later, with Julia obviously pregnant, we gathered in the sanctuary at St. Dominic's for a very small afternoon ceremony in which we were married. Father Deasy officiated. Julia's parents stood with us, as did Bobby from work and his wife. My parents refused to attend, as did my sisters. Afterward, Father Deasy took us to a late lunch, then brought us back to the church and bid us goodbye. We went home to the apartment.

We had no money for a honeymoon and no real inclination to take one. So, we sat at the apartment that afternoon and I did my best to make Julia comfortable. She hadn't been living there before, as had I, and seeing it for the first time as a resident was an arresting experience for her. I admit, the reality of our situation was rather overwhelming, but I was glad to have the wedding done and to put the previous months behind us. At least we were moving forward. Two weeks after that, we bought a refrigerator.

CHAPTER 4

In May, Julia gave birth to our son, David. His arrival seemed a little early by my calculation, but Julia dismissed my concern. When I asked the doctor about it, Julia tried to warn me off with a look, but I asked anyway. He insisted David had arrived right on time, which left me wondering what the look was about.

In the months that followed, I did my best to take care of them—never missed a day of work, took all the overtime the company would give me—but the sense of guilt and shame over getting Julia pregnant and dropping out of school, and of us abandoning our dreams, never left me.

Viewed in the context of the way people live today, it seems rather nostalgic that such a thing as her pregnancy could bother me. People have children together all the time and never marry and never think twice about it, even in the church. But back then, people like us—people who were serious about following the teachings of the church—weren't supposed to do that and it was a big deal that we had, whether we did it on purpose or by accident. I felt nothing but remorse and regret over the way I had conducted myself with her. Constant remorse. Constant regret. Unrelenting guilt. Every moment telling myself I should have been stronger and resisted the temptation to have sex with her. Not that it wasn't fun, and not that I regretted our son, but if I had handled our relationship differently, things might have worked out better. And on top of it all, there was my long-standing desire to become a priest. I had disappointed my parents, Julia's parents, people at college, and myself. And I was sure I had disappointed God.

Not long after David was born, Julia quit her job to stay home with him. Someone had to care for him and paying a sitter to look after him was not an option. Julia enjoyed being with him but with her not working our finances—which had been tenuous before—became impossible. The electricity was repeatedly turned off, and the water, too. There was never enough to eat and never any relief from it. Never any rest.

Desperate to stay afloat, I even asked my parents for help. Mom refused to discuss the matter and Dad scoffed at me. "Your mother and I made it on our own," he said. "No one helped us."

"Pop-Pop helped you get on with the police—"

"You could make it," he snapped, cutting me off. "If you worked hard enough, you could make it." He gave me a snide look. "But that was never one of your strengths, was it?"

Still, I pleaded with him, hoping he might have sympathy

for us, at least for his grandson's sake, but he raised his hand to cut me off. "I didn't bring that squirt into the world," he said. "You're the one who did that. You're the one who has to deal with it."

Julia's parents were no help either. They had been cordial to me when she and I were dating, and even after Julia became pregnant they hadn't been openly hostile, but they were always emotionally distant. When the dire nature of our financial condition became obvious, the anger they'd kept hidden became obvious. Cold anger. Hard anger. They refused to discuss finances with us, and I learned later they began lobbying behind my back for Julia to leave me, using our lack of money as an argument against keeping us together.

Left to struggle on our own, we did the best we could, but it was difficult, even on good days. Our apartment was small, and with David's arrival, it became even smaller. There was little space for the essentials and no space for us to get away from each other. It had no air conditioning and no central heat, which meant it was swelteringly hot in the summer and freezing cold in winter. And it was on the second floor of the building, forcing us to negotiate the stairs for everything. Down and back up to bring in the groceries, take out the trash, and take David for a walk. Down and up. Up and down.

In our second year, the car I bought developed problems that were beyond my ability to fix. Rather than spending money to have a garage repair it, we sold it. Julia and I shared her car, but that was untenable, too. If she needed it for the day, she and David had to get up early and drive me to work. Or I had to arrange a ride with someone on my shift. Or get up very early and walk. Everything was always such a hassle.

After almost a year of that, Julia took a job cleaning offices downtown at night. We alternated our time with David. She looked after him during the day while I worked. I was with him at night while she worked. The extra money helped but our finances were still tight, and we never saw each other except in the kitchen when one of us was going and the other returning. The routine was awkward for me, but it was roughest on her. When she came home in the morning, tired and ready to sleep, David was awake and ready to play. At least when I came home at the end of my day, he was at the end of his and ready for bed.

As we entered our third year together, still with no hope of anything getting better, Julia reached her end. One day, while I was at work, she took David and went back to live with her parents. I learned about it from a note she left on the kitchen table that I found when I came home that evening.

We had no phone in the apartment, so I went to the corner and used a pay phone to call her. Her mother was reluctant to let me talk to her, but Julia overheard the conversation and came to the phone anyway.

"I just can't take it anymore," she said.

"Take what?"

"The cold," she blurted. "The hunger. Never having enough. Never a break. I just can't take it."

"I'm sorry."

"I know." The tone of her voice softened. "I know you don't like it, but I can't do it anymore. I'm done." There was silence for a moment, then, "Goodbye, Jake."

The call ended abruptly, and I slowly returned the receiver to its cradle. Perry's, a neighborhood bar, was across the street and as I stepped from the phone booth, the sign from the bar caught my attention. It was neon, with the tubes bent to form the name in blue, and it glowed brightly against the darkness of the early evening.

Beneath the sign was an open doorway. Through it, I could see the room was dark inside but lights on the shelf behind the bar gave the darkness a surreal effect. The muffled sound of music wafting from the place seemed inviting, too. I had never been inside a bar before, and I had never been drunk, but staring across the street at Perry's, with Julia shutting me out of her life and out of David's, that bar seemed like a comfortable place. A refuge. A shelter. The longer I stared at it, the more inviting it became, and a warm sense of affirmation wrapped around me, drawing me to it. Pulling me closer and closer to the doorway. As if—

"You finished in there?" a voice said.

The sound of it startled me and I glanced around to see someone was waiting to use the phone. I was standing at the door to the booth, blocking his way. "Yeah," I replied. "Sorry. Didn't realize I was—." He pushed past me, stepped into the booth, and closed the door.

Instead of crossing the street to Perry's, I walked back to the building where we lived and climbed the stairs to our apartment. Julia was gone. David was gone. A sense of emptiness came over me. But the thought of that moment on the corner and the way that bar had drawn me toward returned. I pushed it aside, but it lingered in my mind just the same.

Despite Julia's rejection and the abrupt way she left me, I tried repeatedly to convince her to return, but she was tired and afraid, and as the days went by, her parents encouraged her to sever all contact with me permanently. She didn't file for divorce, and she always accepted my phone calls, but after her repeated refusal to meet with me, I stopped trying to make things right.

With Julia and David gone, the balance in my life disappeared. At first, I came home at night to the apartment and stared into the darkness, immobilized by loneliness and guilt. It seemed impossible that things had turned out as they did. I forced myself to do the normal things—eat, shower, wash clothes, get to work—but always beneath a cloud of guilt and the thought that there must have been something I did that drove them away.

Gradually, guilt gave way to depression. I did my best to resist, to persevere, to pull myself up by my emotional bootstraps, but when I could stand it no more, I began to drink. First at Perry's on the corner after work, then at home in the apartment alone. Before long, I had trouble getting to work on time. Then trouble getting there at all. Not long after that, I was fired.

For the remainder of that year, I drifted from job to job, working long enough to pay the rent and a few bills before getting lost in an alcohol-induced numbness. Gradually, I sank deeper and deeper into a stupor that became my constant state. Drunk almost all the time, I stopped eating. I stopped caring. I stopped working. And I lost the apartment.

Alone, and with nowhere else to go, I used the last coins in my pocket to ride the bus to the French Quarter. It seemed like a good option at the time. Tourists. Soup kitchens. Shelters. A part of town where I thought I might be less obvious. Not many members of our parish went there in those days, or so I thought.

At night, I slept on a bench near Jackson Square or in an alley—a few of them were obscure enough to be safe and I seemed to have a knack for finding them. During the day, I ate from plates left by customers at the sidewalk cafés and begged for money on a corner, usually one on Bourbon or Decatur Streets. A few cafés had pay windows that opened onto the sidewalk. I made a note of them and regularly scoured the pavement beneath the windows for loose change.

Whatever money I obtained went to buy alcohol and very quickly I descended into a mindless, unrelenting cycle of sleep, hunger, drunkenness, sleep, interspersed with brief moments of sobriety during which I begged. Needless to say, I lost all contact with Julia, David, and everyone else I had ever known.

CHAPTER 5

Early the next year, or maybe it was the one after that—I lost track of time—my brother-in-law, Marty Lehman, found me and told me my father had died. "Your mother wants you to come home," he said. "For the funeral." I wasn't convinced she wanted to see me, but I liked Marty and he agreed to drive me to the house, so I went with him. I don't know how he found me.

The street outside my mother's home was lined with cars, but the driveway was open. Marty turned onto it and parked his car near the walk that led to the front door. I followed him inside to find the house full of people. Most of their faces were recognizable—cops that Dad had worked with and people from the church—but I couldn't recall the names that went with them, so I smiled and nodded politely. A few of them smiled back but most of them stared at me as if I was an unwashed bum who had come in from the street, which I was but I expected some hint of recognition or a note of civility from them. Instead, I found only disdain and disgust.

My mother, however, was surprisingly hospitable. She came from the kitchen and smiled when she saw me. "Jake," she said in a friendly tone, "you look as if you've been playing in the dirt all day. Go on and get a shower. I've put clean clothes for you on your bed."

From the sound of her voice and the smile on her face, it was as if I was a kid again who had been playing outside and wandered into the house to interrupt one of her meetings—a church committee or the policemen's auxiliary. She didn't care for either of those groups, but occasionally their events were unavoidable. When she had to host them, she did her best to make us appear to be a happy, normal family. Everyone knew we weren't, but still, she did her best to make it seem we were.

That's how she sounded that day. As if I hadn't been away for years, living on the street in a drunken stupor. As if she and Dad hadn't cut off all interaction with me. As if they hadn't left Julia and me to live or die on our own. And as if no one in the room knew how things really were, which they did. It was a surreal moment, but I didn't argue.

After a shower I did, indeed, find clean clothes on my bed. I don't know where they came from, but there they were. Underwear, a dress shirt, casual slacks, a jacket I hadn't seen in years, and shoes. I put them on and joined the others.

The dining table was loaded with food, as was the counter in the kitchen. I nibbled on a few things but tasted them carefully, hoping to avoid an upset stomach. Most of it was heavier than the things I'd been eating.

One thing I couldn't avoid was my need for alcohol and as the afternoon wore on, my hands began to tremble. Marty must have noticed because he ushered me from the house to the backyard. We sat at the picnic table, out of sight from the others, the view from the house blocked by the corner of the garage and a huge pine tree. When we were seated, he took a half-pint bottle of whiskey from beneath his jacket, twisted off the top, and set it in front of me. I added some to the soft drink I was sipping and gulped down half a cup. It felt good, and I had some more. After a third tip of the bottle, Marty took it away. "You can't get drunk," he said. "Not here. Not in front of everyone at your mother's house."

"I just need enough to stop the shaking," I replied.

"Show me your hands."

I stretched out my hands and we could see they barely moved. He smiled and put the cap on the bottle. "You've had enough for now."

The back door to the house opened and Rene came out to join us. We talked about how things had been, and she was pleasant, but I got the feeling she didn't agree with my version of our childhood. "You thought everything was fine?" I asked.

"No," she replied. "I'm not saying that. But we did have a place to live and plenty to eat. And we weren't physically abused."

"I know," I replied. It was true, as I've already admitted. "But their attitude wasn't right."

"Towards you, maybe," she said. "But not toward me and Lorraine."

"Lorraine wasn't here with us when we were in high school." She was eight years older than I was.

"I'm just saying," Rene added. "He didn't make you get Julia pregnant."

That comment cut me deep and I fixed my eyes on her, as she did on me. We stared at each other across the table, neither of us wanting to back down until Marty intervened. "Everyone remembers the life they experienced," he said. "Not the life someone else saw them experience."

Rene glared at him.

"It's the truth," he insisted.

"If you say so."

She rose from her place at the table and flounced inside the house. And right then, I knew she would do everything in her power to cut me out of Mom's life.

As Rene entered the back door, I saw Lorraine, our oldest sister, watching us from the kitchen window. She caught my eye and smiled. I smiled back.

Lorraine was out of high school and in college by the time I was old enough to appreciate her. She attended Tulane but lived on campus and only came home once or twice while I was living there. After graduation, she moved to Chicago. No one said why and I never asked—Mom made it obvious we weren't supposed to—but right then it occurred to me that she might have gone to Chicago for the same reason Julia and I got married.

The following day, we attended Dad's funeral at St. Dominic's. Father Deasy celebrated the Mass. Julia was there with David and we spent a few minutes together, but she refused my invitation for them to join me at my mother's house and offered no invitation for me to join them at hers. I cried on the way back with the others. David had changed so much. I hardly recognized him. He didn't seem to know me at all.

Father Deasy insisted the service at St. Dominic's had to be a traditional Catholic Mass. Mom agreed, but she insisted the burial had to be with police honors. "He was a cop all his life," she argued. "All of his friends are cops. He didn't do anything else but police the city. We can't shut them out." Father Deasy readily agreed.

We buried Dad in St. Louis Cemetery, off Esplanade Avenue. Rows and rows of crypts and statues and all of it filled that day with policemen in their dress blue uniforms. It was quite a sight. So many cops were there I wondered who was patrolling the city. I knew several of them from the street, but they were polite and never said a word to Mom about seeing me in the Quarter. At least, they didn't say anything about it in front of me. Knowing them, they had kept

Dad informed about me right up to the day he died—if he had wanted to know.

After the funeral was over and Dad was buried, we went back to Mom's house and ate. Many of the people who'd attended the service joined us. There was plenty of food and having them help us consume it meant it didn't go to waste. I ate two pieces of chicken, spoke with a few of Dad's co-workers, and retreated to my room.

Once everyone was gone, I went to the kitchen to help clean up. Marty and I washed dishes. Rene and Lorraine packaged the food and put it in the refrigerator. Space in it quickly filled, so one of them brought a cooler from the garage. It smelled like fish, but we used it anyway. Somewhere in all of that, I had a drink and almost had too much, but I managed to keep it hidden, I think.

That night, after everyone else was asleep, Lorraine came to my room and tapped on the door. "Are you awake?" she whispered.

"Sure," I replied, and she came inside.

She sat in the chair at my desk, and I lay in bed, the covers up to my neck. "What's on your mind?" I asked.

"Nothing," she replied. "But it's been a long time since we talked."

"I'm not sure we ever did."

"That time when I drove you home from school," she said. "And we went up to the lake."

"Oh." I suddenly remembered. We walked along the

beach, and she told me about a fight she'd had with Mom the day before. I had been upset by it. "That was a long time ago."

She nodded. "But you remember it?"

"I do now."

"And do you remember what I told you about why Mom and I had been arguing?"

I shook my head. "Only bits and pieces." That was true. I did recall snippets of our conversation, but I had no recollection of what she told me that day.

"Do you remember Johnny Letsos?"

"Yes." My eyes opened wide. "I forgot about him. He used to come over to the house all the time."

"He and I dated through high school," she said. "And that argument I had with Mom—the part that upset you—was the end of an even bigger argument I'd had earlier with her and Dad about me and Johnny. You came home at the end. Dad got angry and left before you got there."

I nodded. It was beginning to come back to me. "He went to that bar where he always went, and Mom had to go get him that night."

"I was pregnant."

"Oh."

"Yeah."

"I guess they didn't like that any better than they liked me getting Julia pregnant."

"Right."

Then I remembered she didn't have any children. "What happened?"

"They wanted me to have an abortion." She began to cry. "But I refused."

"Where's the baby?"

"That summer, I miscarried."

"I don't remember that."

"I wasn't living here," she said. "I was living with Connie."

"Oh. Right." Connie was her best friend in high school. They had an apartment near the Tulane campus for part of the time Lorraine was in college. "How did Mom and Dad react to that?"

Her eyes went cold. "They never said a word."

"They knew you were pregnant, and then you weren't, and they never said anything?"

Her eyes narrowed. "Not a word."

"Do you think they thought you had an abortion after all?"

"Dad said as much later. And made fun of me when I denied it."

"He could be heartless."

"Mom's even worse with the silence. At least with him, you got a reaction. With her, nothing."

"So, how are things now?"

"About that?"

"Yeah."

"I'm okay. It still hurts when I think about it, but I don't think about it too much now. Just once in a while."

"How's Davis?"

"Same as he ever was."

Davis was her husband. He tried to fit into the family, for Lorraine's sake, but the more he learned about how dysfunctional we were, the less time he devoted to it. He was always nice to me, but I couldn't remember the last time I saw him.

"Tell him I asked about him."

"I will."

"What happened with Johnny?"

"He tried to be supportive while I was pregnant, but after the miscarriage, he disappeared. I haven't seen him in years."

"Are his parents still here?" They had been members at St. Dominic's.

"I don't know. I didn't see them at the funeral, and I didn't ask about them." She looked over at me. "I figured Mom wouldn't like it."

"Probably not." But I made a mental note to find out if I had the chance.

The next day, Marty dropped me off at St. Dominic's, and I visited with Father Deasy in the rectory. I was glad to see him, and he seemed glad to see me. We talked as if no time had passed between us. Most of our conversation was about memories from my childhood, my feelings toward my father, and how I thought Mom would handle life without him.

It was a free and easy discussion, but after a while, we exhausted the obvious topics. Neither of us seemed ready to end our conversation, so I said, "Do you remember Johnny Letsos?"

"Ahh." Father Deasy nodded. "You've been talking to Lorraine."

His comment surprised me.

"You know about them?" I asked.

"Yes."

"I didn't remember him until she mentioned him."

"You were young then," he noted.

"Do you know what happened with him and Lorraine?"

"Yes," he replied.

"What was it?"

"I can't say too much. But it was … rather like the situation with you and Julia."

"Except that Lorraine lost her baby."

Father Deasy glanced away. "Well," he said. "That's what she told us." Clearly, he had doubts about Lorraine's version of events.

"You think she did something else?"

"What did Lorraine tell you happened?"

"That she lost the baby. And that Mom and Dad were upset."

"We all were upset," Father Deasy replied. "Some that she lost the child, others that she became pregnant in the first place."

"I assume our parents were upset that she became pregnant."

Father Deasy nodded.

"So, what happened?" I asked.

"Lorraine was a student at Tulane," he said. "When her pregnancy became obvious, it became an issue."

I frowned. "They expelled her?"

"No." He shook his head. "But people started asking questions."

"So, what happened?"

"The girl she was rooming with—"

"Connie."

"Right," he said. "She prepared a tea from cotton root bark and gave it to Lorraine to drink. Several times, I think."

I frowned. "Cotton root? I've never heard of it."

"Cotton root bark," Father Deasy said. "It's a folk concoction that some believed can cause a miscarriage."

"Did it?"

"Apparently so."

He was being unusually cagey, and it was beginning to irritate me. I needed a drink, too, which wasn't helping my attitude. "So, did she have an abortion or not?" I asked. My voice had more of an edge than I expected.

"I'm not sure," Father Deasy said. "She lost the baby,

that much is true. And she had a bad reaction to the tea. But the tea was Connie's suggestion, and I'm not sure how complicit Lorraine was in all of that."

I suddenly felt protective of Lorraine, something I'd never felt for her before. "She was in a tough situation all the way around," I said. "Our parents should have been there for her. Isn't that what parents are supposed to do? Love their children, especially when they mess up?"

"Yes," he said slowly. He seemed to notice I was agitated.

"What about Johnny's parents?" I continued. "How did they take it?"

"They didn't want anything to do with them, either."

Years of anger rose inside me. I did my best to tamp it down, but it was a struggle. "Was Johnny supportive of her?"

"Not really."

"The bastard," I muttered.

"I think Johnny was scared."

No. He was a coward. "So, he abandoned her, too?"

"Not at first."

"But once she lost the baby."

Father Deasy nodded.

"Where is Johnny now?" I asked.

"I think he's living in Orlando."

"And his parents?"

"They're both dead."

"Both of them?"

"They were older," he explained. "Johnny was the youngest by quite a few years."

"Youngest? He has siblings?" I hadn't known that.

Father Deasy nodded. "Two sisters. And a brother. One of the sisters lives in Gentilly." He looked at me intently. "But listen, this was a long time ago."

"Not for me," I snapped. "I didn't know any of this before."

"It was a traumatic time for everyone. Especially for Lorraine. We weren't sure she was going to come through it."

"We?" He'd already said my parents shut her out. "Who else was involved?"

"Your sister Rene."

My eyes opened wide. "Rene was part of this?"

"Rene was with her for the worst of it. Nursed her back to health."

The worst of it. Nursed her. One sister looking after the other. An emotional minefield lay between them. "But not our mother."

Father Deasy shook his head. "She refused."

Knowing Rene was with her back then made me feel better, but it didn't explain the way she acted now. "She and Lorraine don't seem that close," I said. "Something else must have happened."

"After Lorraine lost the baby," he explained, "she still wanted to be with Johnny. She tracked him down. Even moved in with him for a while."

"And?"

"That was a problem for Rene," he said. I could under-stand that. Rene was capable of great kindness, but if she offered advice to someone and they didn't take it, she could cut them off in the rudest way.

There was more I wanted to know about that situation, but by then I had reached my limit of concentration. It was time for me to go and time to find Marty's bottle of whiskey. As I stood to leave, Father Deasy said, "What are your plans?"

"What do you mean?" I knew what he meant, but I couldn't tell him about my plans because I didn't really have any and I surely couldn't tell him I was going back to the street. I didn't want to go back to the street, but I hadn't talked to Mom about staying with her, which was what I wanted to do.

"Jake," he replied, "I've known you since you were born. And I know New Orleans. And I can tell you this: the street has no future for you."

And just like that, I was busted. I looked down at the floor in embarrassment. "How long have you known?"

"Julia's mother keeps me up to date."

A shudder ran through me. I looked up at him. "How does she know?"

He shrugged. "Word gets around."

"I haven't seen her or anyone else in a long time."

"They've seen you," he said with a smile. "More members from our parish go to the French Quarter than you would imagine."

"I suppose so."

"Is that your plan?" he asked. "To go back to the street?"

"I guess. Unless I can stay with Mom."

"Why don't you stay here?"

A frown wrinkled my forehead. "In the rectory?"

"We have a room behind the kitchen in the parish hall," he said. "It's a comfortable place. You could live there. Help the sexton with the grounds. We would pay you. And we have an AA group here. They could help you."

It was a generous offer, especially for a guy like me. A safe place to live and a job. Stability. Emotional support. A chance at a regular life. But after living on the street, I'd become accustomed to experiencing daily life on my own terms. And after being at Mom's house for a few days, I thought there was a possibility I could stay with her and still do as I pleased. "I don't know," I replied. "I was thinking about asking Mom if I could stay with her."

Father Deasy grimaced. "I'm not sure that's a good idea."

"Why not?"

"The dynamics between the two of you are … not good."

He always knew me better than I realized. "Maybe we could work on that," I countered.

"I think it's more likely you'll find the patterns of the past are inescapable without help."

"We'll see." I reached for the door. "I'll let you know."

"Just remember, you can always come back here," he said. "Anytime. No need to call ahead."

CHAPTER 6

Rene and Lorraine stayed at Mom's house for a few days, but by the next weekend, they were gone, leaving me and Mom on our own. Seeing everyone again and not being an embarrassment to them made it seem like things at home had changed with Dad gone. I wasn't glad that he died, but I'm just saying, life at home without him was different and I began to convince myself that I could stay at the house without getting trapped in the way things used to be. Get a job. Settle down again. Live a regular life.

When I broached the subject with Mom, she was open to the possibility. I found work at a restaurant washing dishes and did my best to avoid even the sight of alcohol. Each morning, I rode the city bus to work, and each night I took it home, being careful not to stare out the window at the bars and drive-thru daiquiri shops we passed along the route.

Sober and able to think, hope returned. Before long, I began to wonder if I might yet fulfill my desire to become a priest. Julia and I still were married, but perhaps the church had a vocation for people in my situation. Maybe. And even if not, the possibility of purpose, of a life filled with meaning, renewed my interest in the teachings of the Church. At night, when I returned after work, instead of the things I might have done before, I read Scripture and the Catechism to unwind. Mom seemed pleased by my attitude.

After five or six months of my new routine, things started to feel permanent. I had a place. A life. A future beyond the moment. Then one morning I heard Mom on the phone with Rene. It was a whispered conversation, with an ashtray full of cigarette butts on the table beside her. Not long after that, I saw a realtor's sign in the front yard when I came home from work. I found Mom sitting at the kitchen table and I asked her about it.

"I'm selling the house," she said.

"Why?"

"I'm moving to Baton Rouge to live with Rene and Marty."

"But why?" Everything was going so well for me, and now this. Of all things, this.

"I don't like living here anymore," she said. "The neighborhood's changing. Your father's not here. It's not the same. I don't think it's safe for someone my age."

That was Rene talking. The decision to sell had nothing to do with any of the things Mom suggested. Rene didn't like the fact that I was living with her. That's what it was about. The estate. Their property. She thought I was getting more than my share. Imagining that I was manipulating Mom into supplying me with booze and whatever else her mind dreamed up. She was the one doing the manipulation. Not me. I went to work, came home, studied, went to bed, then did it all again the next day. But I knew that nothing would convince them otherwise. By the next month, the house was sold, and I was on my own.

Frustrated, angry, and bitter, I walked to the bus stop and boarded the first bus going downtown. I was at Canal Street before I remembered Father Deasy's offer of a place to stay, but by then I was resolved to return to my old life. Instead of going to St. Dominic's, I walked over to Bourbon Street and met up with the guys I'd hung around with before. Older alcoholics. Hardcore.

By sunset, time was a blur and after that, one day faded into the next. I can't remember how long I lived like that, but it was a while. Probably a year or more. Begging. Eating from garbage cans in the alleys. Drinking from bottles and cans and cups people threw away before finishing the whole thing. It was a grubby, dangerous existence but most of the time I didn't notice how bad it was because I was drunk.

Then one night I came from a cut-through—one of those passageways between buildings that are about as wide as my shoulders—onto Toulouse Street. It was late. Really late. So late, it was almost early. A dark blue BMW was stopped in the middle of the block. Its brake lights were bright against the darkness, and I stared at them, transfixed by the glow. I was pretty sure the car belonged to Eddie Morrisette, the mayor's son. He posed as just another guy, but he was wired in tight with the drug trade in the Quarter.

A man came from the shadows and approached the car. I heard the electric motor whine as the driver's window on the BMW lowered. My mind went straight to the sound because, even drunk, it didn't sound right. Not smooth like a new one but rough and grinding like it needed replacing soon.

The man from the shadows leaned through the window toward the driver, as if he knew the person inside. Then three gunshots came from the car in quick succession. Bang! Bang! Bang! The muzzle flash lit the area where the man stood, and for an instant I saw his face. It was Pump, a drug dealer.

His real name was Ricardo, but everybody called him Pump. Even the cops. He dealt everything—heroin, cocaine, ecstasy, you name it. Powder, pills, liquid. And pot. Whatever was out there to get a person high, he sold it. I enjoyed talking to him, but I never used anything he sold. It was strictly liquid for me and the one time I bought from him—a bottle of something he called the Side Street Hustle—I didn't feel my fingers and toes for a week. Scared me. I never did it again. He was good for a pleasurable conversation, though, if you caught him in the mornings, just as the night turned gray. That was his best time. Right before sunup. But from the sound of the gunshots coming from the BMW, and from the look on his face, I knew Pump wouldn't see another sunrise.

As the car drove away, I staggered over to where Pump lay in the street. Blood was running from holes in his chest, already forming a red stream that oozed along the grooves between the cobblestones that paved the street. I leaned over him. "Pump. You still there?" His eyes were open and fixed, but I spoke to him again, just to be sure. "Pump, can you hear me?"

When he didn't answer, I knew he was gone. That's when I saw the roll of twenties in his hand. I pried his fingers loose and took the money, then retreated to the shadows and made my way to a store on Rampart Street where I bought a quart of Jack Daniels.

A few hours after Pump was killed—and after I took his money and visited the store on Rampart Street—I was seated on a bench outside St. Louis Cathedral, staring at the curb, watching the shadow from a lamppost as it moved with the rising sun across the sidewalk in my direction. All the while, I was replaying in my mind the things that had happened the night before and feeling guilty about taking Pump's money. I should have left it for the police to find. It might have meant something to them. But they might have taken it, too, and then it wouldn't have made any difference at all. Certainly not as much to them as it did to me.

Somewhere in all of that, I reached for the Jack Daniel's

bottle. It was lying on the bench beside me but when I lifted it by the neck to take a drink, I saw it was empty. Even drunk I knew that was a lot of bourbon for one man to consume and I tried to recall what had happened in the hours since I was at the store with Pump's money, but my mind wouldn't focus on much more than the shadow I'd been watching and the sound of the gunshots coming from the BMW.

After a while, I felt the weight of someone as they took a seat on the bench beside me and when I looked in that direction, I saw Father Deasy. At least, the person seemed like Father Deasy. We stared at each other a moment, me trying to determine if it really was him, and him trying to … I never asked him what he was thinking when he saw me that morning. Then I said, with slurred speech, "You look familiar."

"Yes," he replied with a smile. "I suppose I do."

The empty Jack Daniel's bottle now lay by my foot. He leaned over and picked it up. "Was this yours?" he asked, showing the bottle.

"Yes," I replied. "It was full when I bought it."

"When did you buy it?"

"Last night," I replied.

"So, you drank the entire bottle since last night?"

"Yep," I said. "I drank it all since sunup." That wasn't precisely correct, but I couldn't remember what time I bought it, except that it was after Pump got shot.

"That's not possible," he said.

"I might have had some help," I offered.

It seemed there was someone else with me after I left the liquor store, but I couldn't remember who, or how, or where they came from. I couldn't remember much of anything except the car and the shots and Pump lying in the street with his blood in the grooves between the cobblestones. And the path of the shadow I'd been watching as the sun rose above the buildings to the east. I remembered that, but it was difficult to think of anything else, so I leaned my head forward, rested my chin against my chest, and relaxed.

Sometime later, I felt the bench flex. My head popped up and I saw Father Deasy standing beside me. He took me by the arm and tugged at me. "Come with me," he said.

My eyes opened wider. "Where are we going?"

"To St. Dominic's."

"I know St. Dominic's." I staggered to my feet. "I used to attend there."

He held me firmly by the forearm. "Come on, Jake," he said. "Let's get you away from here."

By the time we reached St. Dominic's, I had sobered up enough to recognize the neighborhood, but it was merely a sense of familiarity. As if I had been there before and nothing more. But when I saw the church, memories from my childhood came back to me and I began to cry. Father Deasy patted me on the shoulder. "It's okay, Jake. We'll figure it out." No one had ever said anything kinder to me, and I cried all the more.

As he had mentioned before, there was a room in the parish hall, behind the kitchen. It had a bed and a wardrobe made from an oversized cardboard shipping box. It was rather stark, but at least it was a room. Father Deasy took me there and put me to bed. I fell asleep immediately.

When I awakened, it was almost nighttime. I sat on the edge of the bed, my head in my hands, and tried to recall how he found me, but all I could remember were the gunshots and Pump lying in the street. Then guilt and remorse swept over me once more for the way I took Pump's money and spent it on a bottle of Jack Daniels. But that didn't take all of the money. What happened to the rest?

My pants were lying on the floor near my feet. I picked them up and checked the pockets. To my surprise, the unspent twenties were still there. What could I—

There was a knock at the door, then it opened, and Father Deasy appeared. "I thought you might be hungry," he said, and he motioned for me to follow. I put on my pants and walked with him to the kitchen. A plate of food was sitting on the counter.

While I ate, he said, "The kitchen is pretty well stocked. You can eat as much as you like."

I took the rest of Pump's money from my pocket and offered it to him. "That's all I have," I said.

He refused. "Keep it," he said. "You might need it for something."

I thought about telling him where it came from and even opened my mouth to speak, but at the last moment I thought better of it and said, "Do you have any clothes I could wear?" Mine were filthy and they stunk.

A bag sat at the opposite end of the counter. I hadn't noticed it until Father Deasy reached for it. "I had to guess at your size." He moved the bag near me. "But I think they will fit."

"Thanks," I replied. It was an inadequate response, but it was all I had at the time.

"There's a washing machine back there." He pointed. "Past the door to your room. After you finish eating, I'll show you how to use it. We can wash the clothes you were wearing."

Our eyes met. "I've made a mess of things," I said.

"You can fix it," he replied. "It won't be as easy as messing it up, but you can put things right."

"But how?" I asked.

"Well," he replied. "To begin with, you can attend our AA meetings."

"I've never been to those."

"Then now's a good time to start."

"Okay. But I meant on a more practical level. Is there something I can do?"

"You mean work?"

"Yes."

"The sexton will have things for you to do," Father Deasy said. "You can talk to him tomorrow."

"What kind of things?"

"There's always grass to mow and appliances that need fixing. I seem to recall you enjoy fixing things."

"Yes." I smiled. "I do." It had been a long time since I had repaired anything, but the memory of a wrench in my hand was a pleasant thing.

CHAPTER 7

As Father Deasy suggested, I began attending AA meetings every Monday evening. Hearing the struggles of others—their frustration with trying and failing and trying again to break free of alcohol and their success at obtaining sobriety—was refreshing and encouraging. During the day, I helped the sexton with lawn care and general repairs around the church, which provided an outlet for my physical energy. Sweating in the Louisiana sunshine was amazingly therapeutic.

Doing all of that required me to follow a normal schedule—awakening in the morning, working all day, sleeping all night—which was something new for me. It was a challenge at first, but the longer I did it, the more regular it became. Sleeping in a bed was difficult at first, too, but as with the routine, I became accustomed to it.

At first, I didn't attend any church services and did my best to hide on Sundays when parishioners came around. Many were acquaintances from my childhood, and some were friends, but I wasn't ready to face them or their questions. Gradually, however, I became aware of my obligation to attend Mass. To satisfy that obligation and to assuage the guilt I felt over my life in general, I began attending the service on Saturday—the Sacrament of Reconciliation. It was the least attended of the regular services. Most people who came to it were serious about living the faith. I thought if someone attending that service knew me, they would be least likely to condemn me for the way I'd lived. Two Saturdays after I started attending, Julia's mother was there. She recognized me but didn't say anything to me, and I didn't try to talk to her. It was a moment, though, and I knew that sooner or later, I had to address the fact that I had a wife and a son…and a mother-in-law.

One day at lunch, after I had been at the church for about a year, Father Deasy took me to a garage near the corner of the property. In a stall next to the one where he parked his car, there was a 1961 Ford Falcon. "The body and suspension are in good shape," he said. "But I don't think the engine runs."

"What's wrong with it?"

"I don't know," he said. "I have a vague recollection that it just quit running one day and no one tried to fix it."

"Whose is it?"

"It belongs to the parish," he replied. "We had it for Sister Elizabeth to drive, but she is no longer with us. She moved to Chicago last year. I don't remember whether the car was working when she left."

"What do you plan to do with it?"

He turned to me with a smile. "If you can fix it, you can have it."

"Really?" I didn't know what else to say. It seemed like an incredible gift.

"Really," he said. "I'm not sure what it will take to get it running, but I'm sure you can figure it out."

Working on the car kept me occupied for several evenings, but there wasn't much wrong with it. Mostly just basic maintenance and a new battery. When I turned the key for the first time, it started right off.

The car was registered in the church's name, which meant the tag had been renewed each year even though the car sat in the garage. Father Deasy helped me get my driver's license renewed, and in a month or two, I was cruising around the neighborhood. It felt good to be free.

At first, I just enjoyed the ability to go whenever and wherever I wanted. Not on a road trip or anywhere of much distance, just to the store, the movies, or the café a few blocks from the church. The effect was liberating. No longer confined to a single location, my life opened up to me in larger terms and I began to think about possibilities rather than limitations. Having a career. And the long-held interest in becoming a priest. Father Deasy was encouraging about all of it except the priesthood.

"There are three vocations," he said. "Do you remember what they are?"

I had studied the Catechism as a child and as an adult and memorized many of the key points. "Single life," I replied. "Married life. And religious life."

"Exactly," he said. "You're not single, you're married."

I sighed. "And that excludes the religious life."

"It excludes the priesthood," he noted. "But it doesn't exclude every religious occupation. There are other things you can do as a married man."

"Such as?"

"Being a sexton is a religious occupation," he offered.

One corner of my mouth turned down in a disapproving look. "I was hoping for something a little closer to the priesthood."

"No occupation is menial in the Kingdom of God. When parishioners arrive for Mass, they appreciate a well-kept lawn. They like toilets that flush. Chairs and pews that are clean. Someone has to take care of those things. Traditionally, that is the job of the sexton."

"I know," I said. "But you know what I mean."

"Yes. I do. And I think the first thing you should concentrate on is your relationship with Julia. Addressing that part of your life will answer many of the questions about what comes next."

"I'm not sure how much I can do to fix things with her," I replied. "I haven't seen her or David since my father's funeral, and they weren't interested in seeing much of me then. David didn't even recognize me."

"He's young," Father Deasy noted. "And he was even younger when she left you. So, he doesn't have much memory of you."

"I saw Julia's mother a few times at confession."

"You didn't tell me about that."

"There wasn't much to tell. I saw her. She saw me."

"Did you talk to her?"

"No. And she didn't talk to me. She and I aren't exactly on speaking terms."

"Did you do something to offend her?"

"I got her daughter pregnant."

"Yeah," he said, stifling a smile. "That would probably affect the way she feels about you."

"I don't know what to do," I continued. "We're still married. We have a son. But it seems rather presumptuous to show up now. I haven't been part of their lives in … years."

"But you're still married."

"We're still not divorced," I corrected.

"But remember, she is just as married to you as you are to her."

I frowned. "Meaning?"

"It's a mutual issue," he said. "It's not just your situation alone."

"I'm not sure they see it that way."

"They?"

"Julia and her parents."

"You could start by meeting her again," he suggested.

"Nothing formal. No expectations. Just being in the same place together. Let her see how different you are now from when she saw you the last time. See where it goes."

"I don't know." It sounded simple enough, but the dynamics with Julia's parents didn't give me much hope.

"You need to figure out what comes next in your life. Your marriage is the place to start. If Julia doesn't want to work things out, you can move forward from there. But you have to start with her." I looked past him, thinking, and after a moment he added, "Would you like for me to arrange a meeting? I know her parents."

"No," I said. "I'll contact her."

A few days later, I drove over to the house where Julia's parents lived and knocked on the door. It wasn't the best way to contact her, but this was in the days before cell phones, and I didn't want to risk someone at the church overhearing my conversation on another line.

Julia's mother glanced out the window and when she saw me her countenance fell, then she disappeared from view. I wasn't sure what would happen next, but the bolt on the lock rattled and the door opened. "Julia doesn't live here now," she said.

"Where is she?"

"They're in Slidell."

Slidell was a town north of the city, on the opposite side of Lake Pontchartrain. I didn't want a fight, so I asked, "Is David with her?"

"Yes," she said coldly. "Where else would he be?"

After Julia got pregnant, I could never choose an approach to her mother that didn't evoke a biting response. "I've been—"

"I know," she said, interrupting. "I've seen you at the church. I know you're working there." Her tone became even more disapproving. "And living there."

"Look," I said, "I'm not trying to start anything. It's just that Julia and I are still married, and I thought she and I should talk. Clear the air or come to an understanding or something. And I haven't seen David in a long time."

Her expression softened. "She's aware of the situation, but I'll tell her you came by." Then she closed the door.

Alone on the front steps outside their house, I thought about all the times I'd been there in the past and the greetings I'd received. Some were friendlier than others, but none as hostile as the encounter I'd just experienced. The pain of it struck deep, bringing to the surface every unfavorable comment Julia's mother had ever made, and then a memory flashed through my mind of a bar two blocks away. The low murmur of customers. Bottles on the shelf with a light shining on them. At the thought of it, a warm, cozy sensation enveloped me, infusing the memory with a sense of acceptance and affirmation. "That's what happens when you encounter a trigger," Hayden Landry, my AA sponsor, called it after I described a similar memory to him. "You have to identify the triggers." Julia's mother certainly fit the description and the sensation I felt from thinking of the bar …

"Take it as a warning," Hayden had said. "When you have a bad experience, and your automatic response is to think about taking a drink, and you have that warm fuzzy feeling just from thinking about it—that experience was a trigger. That warm sensation about drinking, telling you it's okay to have a drink, is a lie. It's not okay to drink. It's never okay to drink. Learn to appreciate that warm feeling as a warning. A confirmation and a warning. Confirmation that the experience you had was a trigger, and a warning that drinking is the wrong response."

An AA meeting was scheduled that evening. It wasn't my usual group, but I attended anyway to make sure I didn't fall into a trap. When I shared my experience with them, they congratulated me on avoiding the urge to drink and I felt good about it, but that's the life of recovery. You're never really cured. You just get better at recognizing the signs of trouble before it starts.

The following spring, I began taking classes at a community college not far from the church. In the first semester, I enrolled in general studies courses, still thinking I might get back to the priesthood. It was a dream that couldn't come true, but one that wouldn't go away so I concentrated on courses in English, history, and math. Subjects I thought would give me better options in the future in case a bigger role in the church opened up.

In the fall, I noticed a poster on a bulletin board about the school's auto mechanics program. A class in history that I wanted to take that semester was full, so I enrolled in a mechanics course as an elective to keep my progress on schedule toward completing a degree in two years. That course proved more interesting than I expected and in the succeeding terms, I took as many mechanic courses as I could fit into my general studies program.

In June, two years later, I completed the requirements for the degree. Father Deasy arranged a reception in my honor. It was held on a Sunday afternoon. He had announced it to the congregation and most who heard about it attended. The parish hall was crowded. I thought Julia's mother might be there. Or maybe even Julia and David. But they weren't. It reminded me of the void that part of my life had become, but I had no way of reaching them other than through her mother, which I already had tried to no avail.

That Sunday evening, after the evening Mass and after everyone had gone home, Father Deasy and I sat in the kitchen on folding chairs and sipped hot tea. It was summertime in New Orleans and even at night the temperature was quite warm, but he liked to drink hot tea no matter the weather, so I joined him.

"I tried to contact Julia through her mother," he said. "About the reception."

"How did she respond?"

"She said she would get a message to her, but I never heard back from either of them."

"Same as before with me."

"Yeah."

"So, what do I do?"

"I think you have to do the next thing," he suggested.

"Which is?"

"You mentioned the priesthood."

"Yes, but with the situation with Julia unresolved that's still not an option, is it?"

"No," he replied. "And I don't think it ever will be. If you're married, you're excluded. If you divorce, you're excluded. So, we should think of this in a different way."

"Like what?"

"Like finding a job for you in a position that involves helping people. That's the core function of a priest. I mean, the catechism speaks of it in terms of discipleship, but there are other ways to do that without ordination."

"But if I'm going to live on my own, I need something with an income that lets me do that."

"Yes, you do."

"Do you think I could make it on my own?"

"Certainly," he said.

"You think I'm ready for that now?"

He nodded. "I think you're ready."

"A job would be good, but I don't know where to look."

"Let me ask around," he said. "I know a few people who might be able to help."

That evening, I lay on the bed, staring up at the ceiling, thinking about what might come next for me and about how the situation with Julia might be resolved. I could drive up to Slidell, ask around, and probably figure out where she lived. If her mother hadn't told her I had asked about her and hadn't told her about Father Deasy's visit—which was very likely the case—then showing up at her door might be effective. But if Julia knew we had asked about her and had intentionally avoided seeing me, then arriving unannounced could lead to a disastrous encounter.

Wrestling with that dilemma brought the matter slowly into focus. There were two options. I could attempt to impose my will on the situation, or I could let it unfold in a different way. God's way.

At a young age, we learned to pray the Our Father—the Lord's Prayer. The first petition of that prayer begins, "Let Your kingdom come, let Your will be done…." Even when I was living on the street, I prayed that prayer every morning and every evening. That night, I prayed it for Julia and David, trusting that God would bring His will to pass in our lives, and did my best to let it rest right there with Him.

Late in July, Father Deasy told me about a job as a shop teacher at Winter Hill Farm, a rehab unit operated with the assistance of Catholic Social Services, at a site near Alexandria, a town in central Louisiana about two hundred miles north of New Orleans. "They need someone to teach their students the basics of using tools. How to get around a workshop. Service equipment. Make simple repairs. No one's expecting them to become master mechanics, but it's a working farm and knowing about that sort of thing is useful. It also keeps them occupied and would give you a chance to relate to them."

"Do you think I could do it?"

"You're handy with tools," he replied. "And you have all those shop courses from college. I think you'll be fine."

"But what about the other thing?"

"What other thing?"

After a long struggle, I was finally holding things together. Moving on seemed like a big risk with that. "Drinking," I said. "Me and alcohol."

"You've moved beyond that," Father Deasy said. "You've learned the discipline of saying no. You did that by taking it one step at a time. Think of this as the next step."

That sounded simple when he said it, but I was afraid of what might happen when it was just me trying to stay sober on my own. Yet maybe he was right. Maybe I was ready for the next thing.

"There's an AA program at St. Francis, a church in Alexandria," he added. "It's not too far from the farm. I know the priest. He's someone you can trust. You could connect with them to help you."

That sounded better. I wouldn't be totally on my own. "What does the program at Winter Hill do?"

"They work with guys who have substance abuse problems. They only take men. And it's a small program. Only about a dozen guys each year. Most of them are your age or younger. They get them off drugs and teach them skills that will help them get on with their lives. Like what you've done here."

"It sounds interesting," I said, intrigued but unsure what I would be getting into.

"It'll give you a chance to start over in another place," he added. "Away from all you've been surrounded with here. And it'll give you some hands-on experience working with people."

"That would be good."

"And you never know where it might lead." He patted me on the shoulder. "Anyway, the job is yours if you want it. Just let me know."

That night, after supper, I went for a walk and thought about Winter Hill and the job and taking that next step. The prospect of working with people who had substance abuse problems was interesting. Certainly, a subject with which I had a lot of experience, though on the abusing side, not the counseling side. And the possibility of being on my own, though scary, was exciting, too. Exciting and scary. I'd been on my own before and ended up living on the street. Sleeping in doorways and eating from trashcans. I didn't want that. But if I was never going to become a priest, the job at Winter Hill might be as close as I could get to that. And that might not be bad. In fact, it might be very rewarding.

But what about Julia and David? Regardless of where they lived or how they felt about me, they were my first responsibility. That was the teaching of the church and my own personal beliefs. Julia remained my wife. David was my son. Was taking the job a choice to distance me from them? Geographically, perhaps. But not emotionally.

And then I remembered something Father Deasy had said. "Think of this as the next step."

A step, not a final destination. There was no way to know what might happen after I arrived at the farm or how long I might be there. All I could do was face the moment in the present context and address the issue at hand on its own merits. Taking the job wouldn't change my relationship with Julia. And if that relationship did change in the future, I could address that situation when it arose.

After two or three circuits around the church property, I found peace in myself about accepting the position and went to bed. When we stopped for lunch the next day, I told Father Deasy I would take the job. He was glad to hear it.

"They want you to be there, ready to work, the first day of September," he said.

He hadn't told me that part before. "That's not far off," I responded. "It's already almost August."

"And you should go up there early," he added. "Give yourself a few days to settle in before you begin."

That made it even sooner than I thought. "So, go up the last week of the month?" I asked.

"Yeah," he replied. "It doesn't give you much time to prepare, but I think that's what you should do."

"That's okay." I grinned. "I don't have much to pack." And it was true, most of my belongings would fit in a single suitcase.

August went by quickly and I had to rush to get ready. The day before I was to leave, Father Deasy found me in the kitchen and invited me into the sanctuary. Our vicar and deacon were present, along with several of the leading men from the parish. We gathered at the altar where they laid hands on me and commissioned me for the job I was about to take. In canon law, it was a consecration, not an ordination, but God was present just the same. I cried when they prayed. Father Deasy did, too.

Afterward, they led me outside to the parking lot where a pickup truck was parked near the sidewalk in front of the sanctuary. It was three years old and in great shape. "We thought a truck might serve you better than a car with this job." Father Deasy offered me a set of keys. "Let's swap vehicles."

CHAPTER 8

Early in the morning, I packed my belongings in the cab of the pickup truck and said a final goodbye to Father Deasy. He had been more of a father to me than my own had ever been and it made me sad to think of daily life without him in it. I think he felt the same about me. He stood in the street and watched until I turned the corner toward a future that seemed both wonderfully optimistic and unimaginably frightening.

At Baton Rouge, I crossed the Mississippi River on a bridge that stood high above the water with a train track running overhead. As I came across from one side, a train came towards me from the other. I was mesmerized by the sight of it. I had never seen train cars from underneath.

When I reached the opposite bank of the river, I turned onto a state road and took it across the river plain towards the interior of the state. The truck had an air conditioner, which was a serious improvement from what I'd been driving, and I'd driven all that morning with the windows up and the air on its coldest setting. The pace on the state road was slower than on the highway, so I lowered the driver's window and drove with my left arm propped on the ledge—with the window down and the air conditioner still on high. The air swirled around me, cool and refreshing, with the sounds of life drifting toward me. It was a comfort I hadn't known in a long time.

Gradually, the road led up from the farmland in the flat by the river to the gently rolling hills of central Louisiana. Miles of woods with deer crossing signs. Pickup trucks pulling boats on trailers. Houses with yards cluttered with children's toys.

Two hours later, I arrived in Alexandria. The directions Father Deasy had given me said I should continue north to Bentley, where I would come to a country store with exterior walls made of brick. "Native clay," he said. "Old style. You'll recognize it. There'll be a rusted Getty Oil Company sign hanging from a pole by the highway. Go past the store and turn right onto the next dirt road."

I found the store without any trouble and steered the truck onto a dirt road that led past more open farmland and plantations of pine with the trees planted in rows, each an equal distance from the others. When I glanced out the side window, they seemed to click by.

A mile or two later, I came to a well-maintained gravel driveway that turned off to the left with a sign that read, "Winter Hill Farm. Private Property," tacked to an oak tree. I followed the driveway through a stand of woods and emerged at the crest of a low hill, just high enough to conceal the buildings that lay below—a rambling farmhouse with white clapboard siding and wide, deep porches that went all the way around, a smattering of outbuildings and a huge, weather-beaten wooden barn. Several trucks and a car were parked near it. A row of equipment—plows, discs, sprayer, hay baler, and one or two I didn't recognize—were lined up against a fence to the right.

The view from the crest of the slope was refreshing and I sat there a moment, letting my eyes scan across the property with the buildings in the foreground, the fields beyond, and a pecan orchard to one side. After a moment, though, I slid my foot from the brake pedal and let the truck roll slowly down the hill, past the house and outbuildings before coming to a stop in front of the barn.

The main doors of the barn were open, and I could see all the way to a catch-pen on the other side and a pasture beyond. Through the darkness of the unlit interior, I saw the outline of a door that opened to the right and beyond it, a shop that was in a separate section with its own doors to the outside.

While I watched, the door to the shop opened and I saw a tractor, its form illuminated by shop lights and the glow from the arc of an electric welding machine. Two workmen were bent over a bar near the tractor's rear axle. Their expressions were earnest but not angry.

I came from the truck, and as I closed the driver's door

a young man appeared. I hadn't noticed him before, but it seemed he'd come from inside the barn. "Could I help you?" he asked.

"I'm looking for Lewis Mitchell," I replied. Father Deasy had given me his name as the person in charge of the program. The director, I think.

The young man gestured over his shoulder. "He's back there. In the office."

It was hot by the truck but noticeably cooler inside the barn as I made my way to the office in the back corner of the building. Lewis was seated at a wooden desk that was cluttered with stacks of files and papers. He glanced up as I entered. "You must be my new guy," he said.

"Jake LaRue," I replied. "Father Deasy sent me."

We shook hands but before we could say anything more, the phone rang. I turned away and stared out the window, pretending not to listen while Lewis took the call. When he finished, he started to explain the program to me, but the phone interrupted us again. From the look of the office and the constant phone calls, it seemed he was running the place by the seat of his pants.

After the fourth call, he took the phone off the hook. "I'm sorry for the interruptions," he said.

"Must be a big challenge to keep this place running."

"I could use five more people just like me," he responded. "But we can't afford them."

"So, tell me what you do up here?"

He had a puzzled expression. "Didn't Father Deasy tell you about us?"

"Yeah," I said. "But I wanted to hear it from you." People will tell you something, and they think they're accurately repeating what they've heard, but it almost never works out to be totally right. I wanted to know what Lewis expected and I wanted to hear it from him.

"We work with men," he said. "No women. And we get most of them from the court. They come to us usually as a condition of probation—if they complete the program, their court case goes away. Almost all of them have substance abuse problems. Alcohol and drugs, mostly. Occasionally we get someone who fried their mind sniffing glue or gasoline or drain cleaner. Not much we can do for them, but the others we can help."

I knew people from the street who fit his description. Old-timers who drank their life away. Young guys who wasted their bodies on meth. And the desperate ones who snorted inhalants from aerosol cans or gas fumes from the tank of a car. A guy who hung around Rampart Street once stole a string of balloons from a vendor just to inhale the helium from them.

"What kind of staff do you have?" I was trying to say something that sounded intelligent. That was the best I could come up with.

"The students are housed in that farmhouse you passed on the way in. Two group leaders live with them. Doug and

Mike. We have a cook, Howard, who prepares their meals. George Blaney, the farm manager, keeps everything running. He lives down the road."

"You have a farm manager?" Father Deasy told me it was a working farm, but I hadn't thought of it as a real farm.

"This is a farm," he replied. "We expect to turn a profit from it."

"What's the routine like?"

"Students attend shop classes in the morning, learning things like carpentry, welding, auto mechanics. We try to teach them the basic skills necessary to operate a place like this. Hopefully, in the process, they figure out what they're going to do once they get out of here."

"Is that all the education they receive?"

"No. And we're not running a vocational school. Most of what we do here is done with the ultimate aim of putting the students in a situation where they can confront the underlying issues that caused their problem in the first place. Anger, resentment, bitterness on the surface. Fear, abandonment, lack of purpose underneath. Work applies enough stress to bring all of that out."

"And when it does, what do I do?"

"Duck," he quipped. I waited for him to continue. "If it's serious, tell the group leaders or me. Otherwise, deal with them the way you would if you were talking to a friend."

"Or a son?"

"Sort of, but don't get too involved with that part of it.

We have counselors to keep them on track. They'll come to you in the mornings. You'll teach a shop class. After that, a tutor works with them on lessons designed to prepare them for the GED examination. Most of these guys don't have a high school diploma. That's the first step in making them employable. When they finish with that part of the day, they go to work."

"Work?"

"Like I said, Winter Hill is a working farm with livestock, crops, the whole deal. All of it requires constant attention. Especially in the summer and fall. And these guys need to learn how to work, and we give them an opportunity to do that."

"The students are your labor force."

"When they come to us, most of them know nothing about how to work, how to keep a job, how to get through a workday. We help them figure that out. And, like I said, the stress of manual labor gives the group leaders opportunities to engage their underlying issues. You'll see how it works as we go, but I need you to focus on the shop. The last guy we had didn't really do much with them. Spent most of his time creating art from scrap iron. The students just sat around and watched. We want them to get their hands dirty and learn something."

"What ages are they?"

"Rick is the youngest. He's eighteen. Reuben McKay is twenty-nine. I think he's the oldest." Lewis stood. "Come on.

I'll introduce you to everyone."

We left the office and walked through the barn to the main doors, then across the compound to the house. Some of the students were in the living room with Doug; others were in the dining room with Mike. Lewis introduced me to them and the tutor, Jessica Patterson, a student at Northwestern, a state school up the road in Natchitoches. They were polite, but the situation felt awkward.

When we were outside again, I said, "Father Deasy suggested I would be working with the students in a way that was more like mentoring than merely teaching them skills."

"I need you to stick to the shop work," Lewis said. "You'll see. This is best. Doug and Mike know what they're doing. It's all about discipline with these guys, not much about nurturing, growing, relating. These students need discipline and structure. A lack of that is part of the reason they wound up in trouble. Doug and Mike can handle that. You need to handle the shop."

We'd been walking back to the barn and came to a stop beside my truck. "You'll be living in a farm worker's cottage at the far side of the property," Lewis said. He handed me the keys to the house and told me how to find it. "The students will be here in the morning, ready to go at nine. You should get here before that." Then he turned away and disappeared inside the barn.

After talking to Lewis and after meeting Mike and Doug and the students, I was more uncertain than ever about whether I could work at Winter Hill. The reality of it was more real than I'd imagined. And the expectation that I would actually do something seemed overwhelming. Life on the street had acclimated me to living with no expectations. But, having nowhere else to go at the moment, I drove to the worker's cottage. "At least I can spend the night," I mumbled to myself. Slipping away without saying goodbye seemed like a viable option, too.

The cottage was better than I expected, with two bedrooms, two bathrooms, and a combined living room and kitchen. On the end opposite the kitchen, there was a fireplace with a sofa and an overstuffed chair. A picture window along the wall to the left offered a view of a pasture, with a grove of sparsely spaced oak trees to the left and an open field to the right.

Thankfully, the house was air-conditioned, and I turned the setting down to make the room comfortable, then unloaded my belongings from the truck. That didn't take long and when I was done, I found the coffee pot, then settled into the chair by the fireplace with a cup of afternoon coffee.

While I sipped coffee and stared out the window, a cow appeared, loping toward the trees. Three more followed. Their pace was deliberate but unhurried, methodically placing one hoof in front of the other until they reached the darkest, coolest part of the shade where they lay down. Content and unbothered, their jaws moved in that unconscious side-to-side motion that cows use to grind their cud. Their tails lazily swished away the flies that landed on their backs.

Another sip or two, and my mind wandered from the scene outside to images from my life that brought me to where I was that day. Serving as an altar boy at St. Dominic's. At home, in the living room, trying to get my father to like me. Following my mother through the kitchen, wondering why she didn't take up for me when he yelled at me. Seeing Julia's smile when we were young. My father's derisive comments when I told him she was pregnant. Working at the coffee plant. That tiny apartment and the day Julia left. Living on the street, then with my mother, then on the street again.

Family relationships were a struggle for me. Wanting but not wanting. Having but not having. A sense of loss over things never experienced. A sense of reluctance about trying. It was odd. My parents didn't treat me like other parents treated their children. I knew classmates who were beaten regularly, sent to bed hungry, punished with cigarette burns on their arms and backs. Mine didn't treat me that way, but they didn't treat me like the good parents treated their children, either. They didn't beat me or lock me in a closet, but they weren't supportive of anything I tried to do. When I wanted to play baseball, they wouldn't pay for a glove. When I wanted to play basketball, they refused to buy shoes. When

I decided to attend college, they did nothing to help. Father Deasy found people to support me. My parents didn't even drive me to the bus station. I had to get there on my own. Julia took me.

When I decided to take the job at Winter Hill, it never occurred to me that I should tell my mother I was leaving New Orleans. Maybe I would send her the address later. A card. Or a letter. Maybe. But probably not. If she needed to find me, Marty could figure out how to reach me. And if things happened and I didn't know about them, that's just the way it was. I know I wasn't supposed to feel that way, but I had learned from Father Deasy and the guys in our AA meetings that honesty was important and, honestly, I didn't care to be around them or for them knowing much about me.

My cup was empty, so I refilled it and returned to the chair. By then, two more cows had joined the others in the shade. It was a peaceful scene—the trees, the shade, the cows—but I knew from being at the barn that it was miserably hot out there. And I knew from what I'd seen and heard so far, working at the farm would be a challenge for me.

To begin with, there was no curriculum for a shop class—a fact that became clear to me while talking with Lewis—and I had never taught a course to anyone about anything. Which meant I would arrive at the barn in the morning with a dozen guys looking to me to tell them something they didn't know. But what could I teach them? This is a screwdriver? This is a hammer? That hardly seemed like something anyone would be interested in.

For a moment, it seemed as if I was staring into a deep, dark abyss. And then I remembered my first day in my first class in auto mechanics. That's exactly what the instructor, Steve Lloyd, did. He began by asking about the parts of a car, starting at the front. What's this? A bumper. What's this? A fender. When he'd gone all the way around the car, he moved to the workbench and did the same thing with the basic tools. Someone scoffed at him for it, and he said, "If you don't know the basics, you can't learn the complex."

"That's what I'll do," I said to myself. "I'll do what Steve did."

The next morning, I awakened early. Someone had been kind enough to stock the refrigerator before my arrival and I prepared a breakfast of scrambled eggs and toast, then ate it at the kitchen table with a cup of coffee.

Since Father Deasy had rescued me from the street, my mornings had begun with Mass. He recommended I attend services at St. Francis in Alexandria, but that was thirty minutes away, too far to attend every day. So, that first morning on the farm, I read a few pages from the catechism and the first chapter of the Gospel of Mark, intending to do that every morning until I could figure out a better routine.

When I finished reading, I poured myself another cup of coffee and thought about the job and how I needed to stay and make the best of it. Father Deasy had recommended me for it, and I didn't want to let him down, but even more than that, I needed to do it for myself. I'd been starting and stopping a lot since leaving college. It was time to see something through. "I'll give it a chance," I said to myself. "Maybe I can help these guys with some of the experiences I've been through."

Rather than waiting at the cottage until closer to nine, worrying about what the day would be like and struggling with whether I knew what I was doing, I drove to the barn and arrived almost two hours ahead of schedule. Even at that hour, a light was on in the office, and I found Lewis seated at his desk. Files for the students were kept in a locked cabinet in the corner of the room. He opened it for me, and I took the files to a table near the door where I sat and read. There were only twelve students in the program, but most of them had files that were thick with documentation from court appearances and notes from counseling sessions. After an hour of that, I filled out the usual employment forms, then walked over to the shop and prepared for class.

Around nine, the students arrived for our first session together. The shop was dirty and cluttered, so I put them to work sweeping it, then had them clean every tool, organize every workbench, sort through the contents of every cabinet. As they did that, I asked them questions about the tools, as a way of seeing how much they knew. The students were unenthusiastic.

"We know the names of the tools," Pete Romero groused. "Hammer, screwdriver, pliers."

"And we don't care about the others," someone added.

Their comments didn't sit well with me, but I avoided the urge to remind them that I was the teacher and they were the pupils. A compression sleeve lay on the workbench near where I was standing. I held it up for them to see and glanced over at Pete. "What is this?" I asked.

He shrugged. "It's a thing you use to do something with."

Everyone laughed.

"But what is it called, and what is the thing it does?" I asked.

"I don't know," he replied.

I glanced around at the others, still with the sleeve in my hand. "Does anyone know what this is?" When no one answered, I said, "It's a compression sleeve. It's used to compress the rings on a piston so you can slide the piston into the cylinder of an engine." They all had blank expressions, so I continued. "Does anyone know what a piston is?"

Frank, another of the guys, reached into a cabinet and took one out. "One of these?" he asked, holding it up.

"Yes." The piston was worn and cracked, but I took it from him and held it as an exhibit. "This goes into the cylinder of an engine."

Palmer, a guy from Metairie, spoke up. "What kind of

engine are you talking about?"

"An automobile engine," I said. "Or a truck engine." We needed an engine to use as a teaching aid and I made a mental note to find one. "Does anyone know what a cylinder is?"

Pete spoke up. "It's the round hole."

"Yes," I said. "In a typical automobile engine, there are eight cylinders with eight pistons." That was true at the time. Things have changed some since then.

"What difference does it make?" Alan asked. He was from Morgan City, on the Atchafalaya River, a gateway to the Gulf for fishermen and oil rig crews.

"Yeah," Ron added. "Why do we need to know any of this?" He was from Opelousas. His father was in the timber business. I was amazed I could remember even that much detail about them in such a short time.

"We live on a farm," I explained. "We use equipment all day, every day. Sometimes, that equipment needs to be repaired."

"So, the more we know," Pete said, "the more valuable we become. And the more work we can do."

They all nodded and murmured. Gary, a new guy from Baton Rouge who was standing on the opposite side of the shop, said, "We're nothing but slaves."

"You're not slaves," I replied.

Dillon, a stocky guy with a winsome smile, laughed. "We work and don't get paid for it, don't we?"

"We get a place to live," Frank replied.

Dillon was dismissive. "I could get that on the outside with a lot less trouble."

"If you could get that on the outside," Pete said, "you'd be on the outside."

The remark seemed to anger Dillon. "How about I stuff your head in the—"

"Listen," I said, cutting them off. "You're here. Okay? This is what we do. You need to learn this stuff."

While the students sorted and cleaned the shop, I tried to talk to Pete about his plans for the future. His file indicated his father was in business. I thought he would be someone who was thinking about the future. My attempt was awkward and forced, but I wanted to try and so I did.

"All I'm interested in is doing my time and moving on," he said. "Twelve months here is better than twelve months in prison. That's the option they gave me, and I took it. When I get out, I'm going home. My old man will find something for me to do. So, talk to somebody else about what they're going to do. I'm not interested."

Dillon was standing nearby. "If you're trying to get us to talk, it won't work. No one opens up to anyone," he said. "If you talk, whatever you say gets used against you in a group meeting." Group meetings, I learned later, were the way they resolved differences among the students.

Frank spoke up. "Hey, what's this?" He was holding a tool that looked like a metal clamp, but it had a knob on one end and some extra pieces.

"That's a micrometer," I replied. "You use it to measure the thickness of something. Steel. Wood. Whatever." I took it from him and clamped it over a board on the workbench, then turned the dial on the handle until it was tight and pointed. "The part you twist is called a thimble. When it's tight, you read the numbers on the handle, and it tells you how thick the piece is. This one is .257 inches."

Frank grinned. "That's cool. Can I try it?"

"Sure." I handed it to him, and he spent the morning measuring the thickness of everything in the shop. I didn't mind. At least he was interested.

Later that morning, Jessica, the tutor, arrived to work with the students. She parked her car near the house. I watched from inside the barn as she made her way inside. Her arrival signaled an end to shop class, and the students dutifully trooped up the hill to study with her.

When they were gone, I busied myself servicing a tractor for George, the farm manager, and a truck they used to haul corn to a grain elevator in Tioga, a nearby town. Doing that kept my hands busy, but my mind thought about the students and how I could engage effectively. They'd had a sullen attitude that morning, but I suspected it wasn't all attributable to disinterest. Maybe they weren't interested in merely keeping busy or in gathering information solely for the sake of having information. Whatever I did with them needed context. Something that gave purpose and meaning to the content I was trying to convey. Purpose. Meaning. Value. A project. They needed a project. That way, they would learn without knowing they were learning. But what kind of project?

By the time I finished the work for George, it was lunchtime. I ate with the guys at a table on the back porch of the house. Country fare. Beans, potatoes, chicken, cornbread. And sweet iced tea. Howard, the cook, knew how to prepare comfort food, and the guys knew how to eat it. I did, too.

When we finished, they went inside for more study, then to work in the field. I returned to the shop. Sometime that afternoon, Frank showed up at the shop. "George said he didn't need me. Told me to come help you."

"What are the other guys doing?"

"Getting ready to pick the corn, I think."

It was August, the last month of summer. Not a time of year I associated with harvesting. That was something for autumn. And we were in Louisiana. The weather wouldn't feel like autumn until late October or November. But if George thought the corn was ready, who was I to question him? Until coming to Winter Hill, I had never worked on a farm for even a single minute.

Servicing the equipment earlier in the day had left an oily mess on the shop floor. We needed to clean it up. "Why don't we—"

A noise interrupted us—the sound of a car trying to start

but failing. I glanced through the doorway, searching for the source. Frank noticed my reaction. "What is it?" he asked.

"I'm not sure."

From the doorway, I saw Jessica's car was parked at the house. At first, I thought it was unoccupied, but then I saw her hunched over the steering wheel as she turned the key again to start the engine, but it didn't catch. Frank saw her, too.

"Does her car always act like that?" I asked.

"I don't know," Frank replied. "I never paid much attention."

"Come on."

He followed me from the shop, and we walked up the hill toward the house. Jessica was still sitting behind the steering wheel as we came alongside the driver's door. "Does it have gas?" I asked.

"Yes." She pointed to the gauge on the dash as proof.

"Pop the hood latch," I said.

She pulled a lever beside her seat, and the latch disengaged. The hood came free, and I raised it, then looked around at the engine. The wires seemed to be in place, so I caught her eye and said, "Try it again."

She turned the key, but the engine still wouldn't start. I had a screwdriver in the side pocket of my work pants and used the handle of it like a hammer to tap an electrical box mounted on the fender. "Try it now," I said.

The engine started, and I closed the hood. She shouted

out the window to say thank you but drove away without waiting for me to respond. I watched until she topped the hill and disappeared.

As we walked back to the shop, Frank asked, "How did you know to do that?"

"Know to do what?"

"Hit that box."

"It looked like the thing to hit," I replied.

We both laughed.

CHAPTER 9

As a first attempt at a project, I tried to interest the students in building new cabinets for the shop. Jose ruined several pieces of wood, and Dillon clobbered his fingers with a hammer. Rick, somehow, stabbed himself with a screwdriver, and Gary cut himself with a saw. He was quite melodramatic about it, screaming and moaning and flailing around, but when I checked, I saw it was only a nick. The others laughed at him for making such a fuss.

In the midst of that, George arrived on a tractor pulling a potato digger—a massive piece of equipment with chains and sprockets and dozens of moving parts. The digger was a mess with dirt and weeds and rotten potato vines all over it. He dropped it on a concrete pad beside the shop. "It needs to be cleaned and greased before we park it for the winter," he said. "Been sitting out there by the field since May. We don't start digging again until next May, but it can't sit like this 'til then." The farm, I learned later, grew two hundred acres of potatoes for table stock, the kind sold in grocery stores and fruit stands.

When George was gone, Pete looked over at me. "See." He had an accusing tone as he pointed to the digger. "This is what we've been telling you. We're just free labor for them."

"Well, it's not free," I replied. "They do feed, clothe, and house you."

He scowled at me. "So now you're on their side?"

"Yeah," Rick chimed in. "We thought you might be different."

They'd already shown they could be impossible at times, and I had decided not to argue with them. "We have a job to do," I said. "So, let's get it done."

"What does that mean?"

"It means, get the power washer and get busy." I spoke in a commanding tone, though I wasn't angry.

Reuben came from the shop with the washer. He and Dillon connected it to a water hose, then Reuben climbed onto the digger and began washing away a season's worth of dirt. After thirty minutes, he gave the task to Dillon, then Gary took a turn.

When it was Pete's turn to run the washer, he climbed atop the equipment, then aimed the wand at the others who were standing on the ground and began spraying them. They howled and shouted and tried to climb up to him, but Pete laughed and turned the nozzle to a solid stream, which he directed toward them as if it were a gun. In the calamity that followed, they were all drenched and muddy. Pete stood with his arms raised like a champion, then turned the sprayer on them once more.

I walked over to the machine and switched it off. "What has happened to you guys?" I demanded.

"Nothing," Pete retorted. "We just ain't gonna take the crap you dish out."

"What crap?"

"Learn a skill. Get a job. Build this. Clean that. It's not the kind of training that will lead to anything. It's just what they tell us to convince us to do their work for them. All they want is free labor to run their farm."

I gestured to the digger. "It's your turn. Do it right."

Pete glared at me.

"Okay," I said. "Then try this. You're here under a court order. If you don't want to participate, you can always go to jail."

Pete conceded. "You know, you can only come from that authority thing so many times."

I switched on the washer. "Just clean the equipment and get it over with."

Pete turned to the task at hand, working his way methodically down the machine. The others joined in, pulling weeds and vines from the sprockets. They worked all morning on it, then Pete and Frank returned in the afternoon to finish the job.

As they cleaned up afterward, Pete said, "I'm sorry for my attitude earlier."

"That's okay," I replied. "You did the job in the end."

"It's just that you're a lot like my father. Always telling me what to do. Get busy. Straighten up. Become somebody. As if I'm not somebody already."

That aggravated me. The last thing I wanted was to be like anyone's father. Certainly not my own. "I didn't mean it that way," I said.

"That's how it sounded."

Before I could say more, Frank said, "At least you know who your father is. I don't even know my father's name." From the file, I had learned that Frank's mother was a prostitute who worked the streets in the French Quarter. I probably had seen her from time to time but didn't know it.

"Yeah," Pete groused. "I know my father's name, but he was never around when I wanted him to be. Always at the office or on the golf course. And when he was around, he was always on my ass about doing more."

They were quiet a moment, then Pete looked over at me. "So, what about you?" he asked.

"What about me?"

"What was your father like?"

"He was a cop from New Orleans," I replied.

Pete chuckled. "I bet that was strict."

"He wasn't much of a father."

"How'd you get here?"

"I ended up an alcoholic living on the street," I explained. "A priest rescued me. Helped me get straightened out. Told me about a job at this place."

"So, you're just like us," Frank said.

"Yeah." I grinned. "I guess I am."

"And I guess you're into all that religion stuff, too," Pete noted. "They try to get us interested. Just more of the stuff they tell us. But I'm not buying that, either. I only go to church because they make us."

"Well," I replied. "I'm not into religion, but I do attend Mass every week. Used to go every morning."

"Every morning?"

"Yeah."

"How is that not religious?"

"I don't go to conform to a religion. I go because it helps me keep things in their right place."

"You still go every day?"

"Not since I came up here. But there's a church in Alexandria I was thinking of trying."

Frank spoke up. "St. Francis?"

"Yeah," I said. "You know it?"

"That's where they take us every Sunday," he said.

Pete was about to say something, but Frank continued. "I used to go to Mass with my mother. We went to St. Louis Cathedral."

"And what good did that do you?" Pete responded.

"I don't know." Frank shrugged. "But it always made me feel better."

They worked with me until dinner time. Pete left the shop

as soon as we were through, but Frank lingered. "Think they would let me ride with you to Mass one morning?" he asked.

"I don't know. I'll have to check."

"Okay."

When he was gone, I closed the shop and walked over to Lewis' office. "How's your first week going?" he asked.

"Getting organized. Getting to know the guys."

"That's good."

"A few of them seem to be getting comfortable with me. They're starting to talk a little more."

"Just remember," he cautioned, "your job is to teach. We have group leaders to do the counseling."

I resisted the urge to argue. "Frank asked about going with me to Mass in the mornings."

Lewis winced. "I don't think so. We take them to Mass on Sundays. That's enough."

"He's interested," I responded. "And he actually wants to go."

Lewis had an exasperated tone. "Look, I appreciate what you're trying to do, but just stick to teaching in the shop. Leave the counseling to Doug and Mike. These guys need to learn to work. If they'd been able to hold a job, they wouldn't have gotten into trouble in the first place. That's the part we need you to help with. Teaching them to work. Doug and Mike will look after the other stuff."

I wasn't giving up. "But he wants to go," I said. "Isn't that the point? To get them to want to change. I think it would make a difference for him."

Lewis gestured in frustration. "Okay," he sighed. "But he's your responsibility. Anything happens, it's on you."

Early the next morning, I picked up Frank outside the house where the guys lived, and we drove to Alexandria. On Jackson Street, we passed a woman walking along the sidewalk. She seemed familiar and Frank said, "That looks like Jessica."

"Why would she be out here?"

"She lives in Alexandria."

"But it's early."

"Probably going home."

I brought the truck to a stop, put it in reverse, and began backing up toward her. "Home from where?"

"Been out all night, I imagine," Frank said.

"She lives like that?" I asked.

Frank nodded in response.

"How do you know that?" It seemed so inconsistent with my expectations for what life outside New Orleans was really like.

"When y'all aren't around, she spends the afternoon sleeping."

"Sleeping?"

"Pete wakes her up if someone's coming. Him or Dillon."

Frank gave me a look. "But don't say anything about it."

"Why not?"

Frank stared out the window. "Because they'll know I talked if you do."

We were alongside her by then. I brought the truck to a stop and gestured for Frank to open the door. "Let her in," I said.

He opened the door and smiled at Jessica. "Need a lift?"

"Yeah," she replied. "Thanks."

When she was seated between us, I asked, "Where are you headed?"

"There's a store up the street." She pointed. "I'll show you."

I put the truck in gear, and we started forward. "Do you live around here?"

"Yeah."

From the tone of her voice, it seemed obvious she didn't want to talk, so we rode in silence. Three blocks up the street, we came to a convenience store. She pointed to it, and I stopped the truck in the parking lot. Frank opened the door to let her out. "Thanks," she said.

We watched as she walked into the store, then I steered the truck back to the street. As we continued on our way toward the church, I glanced over at Frank. "Reckon she really lives around here?"

"From what I hear."

"I thought she was in school at Natchitoches."

"She was," he replied, "but she dropped out earlier this year." That was news to me, but I decided not to press the issue any further right then.

We attended Mass at St. Francis and met Richard Brennan, the priest. He and Father Deasy were friends, and I wanted to make myself known to him. Afterward, Frank and I drove back to the convenience store where we'd dropped off Jessica earlier. It was on our way to the farm, and I wanted a cup of coffee.

To my surprise, Jessica was behind the counter working as the store's cashier. When we picked her up, I had assumed she was going there to buy something. Learning that she worked there cast her situation in a different light. I wanted to know more about her situation, but the store was busy with early morning commuters. All of them seemed to want a biscuit and sausage. Frank did, too, and we had to wait in line to get ours and ate it in the truck as we rode back to the farm. But I thought about Jessica all the way. Not romantically but about her situation. It reminded me of life in the apartment with Julia after we married and the sense of desperation that hung over us. Desperation like that does something to a person, and I wondered what it was doing to Jessica.

In the afternoon, back on the farm, George sent Alan, Norm, and Rick to work on clearing a path through the woods for a new fence. He gave them a farm truck to use. Frank worked with me in the shop. Before we had accomplished very much, I glanced through the doorway and saw Jessica coming from the house. I assumed she was leaving for the day, but in a moment, she appeared in the shop.

"So, you saw me at the store," she said.

I wanted to know the truth of her situation, so I asked. "Are you really a college student?"

"Yes." She glanced nervously at Frank. "Well, no. I mean, I was, but I dropped out."

"Why?"

"If you must know, I got pregnant."

"Oh." I looked at her stomach, unable to avoid checking. "When are you due?"

"I already had the baby."

That didn't seem to fit with what I thought Frank told me. "So, you got pregnant … last year."

"Yeah," she said. "It's a long story."

I propped against the workbench. "Go ahead. I have time."

She sighed. "I came to Northwestern last year with my boyfriend. We've known each other since sixth grade. He wanted us to live together. My parents were paying for school for me, so I figured out a way to get them to pay the housing cost for the year. Then I dropped out of the dorm and got a refund on the dorm fee, which I used to pay for an apartment. Then I got pregnant."

Guilt. Shame. Despair. I had lived the scenario she described, and for an instant, the pain of it struck deep in my soul, but I pushed it aside. "And what did your parents say about that?" I asked.

"When I got pregnant, they stopped paying for school and told me I was on my own."

I knew the feeling of that, too. "Where's the baby?"

"She's at home with my boyfriend."

"What's he doing?"

"He's still in school."

"And you're the one paying his bills?"

"I work here and at the store."

"And your boyfriend?"

"He doesn't have time to work and go to school, too."

That didn't sit well with me—boy gets girl pregnant, girl disrupts her life to pay bills, boy continues living same as before—and I was ready to say so, but she spoke first.

"Look," she continued. "I shouldn't be telling you all this. It's none of your business. I just don't want you to say anything to anybody here about it. Please. I need this job."

Despite identifying with her situation, I was suspicious of the boyfriend, and of her. "This morning, when we picked you up, you were walking. And you said your boyfriend had the car. So, if he went to class and you went to work, where was your baby?"

"Look, I'm trying to do the right thing." Her voice was tense, and she gestured with both hands when she talked.

"Where was your baby?"

"I'm doing the best that I can," she said.

I was determined to get an answer. "Who looks after the baby when your boyfriend is in school and you're at work? Or when he stays out all night and you're at work?"

Jessica glanced away. I pressed the point. "Jessica, where does the baby stay if you're not there and he's not there?"

"She stays by herself," she mumbled.

"By herself?" I knew that would be her answer, but hearing it left me astounded.

"It isn't long. Not more than an hour or two." Tears filled her eyes. "She can't walk yet. She stays in the baby bed."

"By herself?"

"I give her a bottle before I leave and some Benadryl. She sleeps the whole time. Most days, she's still asleep when I come back."

George entered the shop. Jessica looked apprehensive. I smiled at her. "So, have you had any more trouble with the car?"

"No," she replied. "It's running all right now."

"Good," I said. "Let me know if it needs more attention."

I didn't wait for her response but walked past her toward George. "How's that potato digger looking?" I asked.

"Looks clean," he replied. "But there's a couple of rollers that need to be replaced. I forgot to tell you about them when I brought it in yesterday."

I had no idea what he was talking about, but it seemed like a chance to get him away from the shop. "Show me," I said, and we walked to the potato digger together.

As George showed me the parts that needed replacing, I glanced toward the field and saw a farm truck bouncing through the grass. Alan, Norm, and Rick were seated in front, with Alan behind the steering wheel. Suddenly, the truck spun around in a circle, and I could see through the windshield they were laughing and having fun.

Teenagers, I thought. Some things never change.

CHAPTER 10

The next morning, I picked up Frank at the house and we went to Alexandria for Mass. Afterward, I sent him to the truck while I told Father Brennan about Jessica's situation and her need for daycare. At first, he seemed to think I might be the child's father, but I assured him that was not correct. "She needs a place for the child during the day," I said. "Can she bring the baby to the parish daycare?"

"Yes," Brennan replied. "But we have a policy that all parents must pay a minimal fee. We have found from experience that unless they pay something, they won't participate regularly. We want the parents involved on a continual basis. The children need it."

I felt certain there was more to it than that, but I was in no position to argue with him. "How much is the fee?"

"Fifty dollars per week," he said.

"Does it have to be paid by the parent?"

"No. I just mean, there's a weekly fee. We have to show that they are participating." He gave me a knowing look.

"Ah. The parish council." The council set the policy for

the parish. I had heard from Father Deasy that they sometimes could be contentious.

"They make the rules," he said. "I try to keep them satisfied."

I had some money Father Deasy had given me to cover my expenses until I got set up with the job, so I took a fifty-dollar bill from my wallet and handed it to him. "That will cover the first week," I said. "She'll be here tomorrow. Don't tell her I paid."

He frowned. "Are you sure this isn't your child?"

"She's not mine," I answered. "I'm just helping out." I turned to leave, then hesitated. "I was once in this position and no one helped me, except Father Deasy."

He smiled. "Deasy is a good man."

"Yes, he is."

In the shop later that morning, I noticed Rick seemed listless and tired. Dillon dozed off frequently, too, and Norm kept sucking on an orange, which was odd because no one had ever brought food to the shop before. When he finished with it, he tossed the orange into a trashcan near the table saw.

When the students left to study with Jessica, I retrieved Norm's orange from the trash. The peeling was still intact, but the stem had been removed and there was a dime-sized opening cut in its place. Through it, I could see the inside was still damp with juice. I had my suspicions about what it all meant, but I needed someone to confirm it for me.

Holding the orange in my hand, I walked across the compound to a large fuel tank where George was filling a tractor. I offered him the orange and asked, "What do you make of this?"

He glanced down at it, then said, "It's an orange. Is that a hole in the top?"

"Yeah."

"Then I'd say someone sucked the juice out of it."

"I know, but there's still a little in it. Taste it and tell me what you think." I offered it to him again.

George frowned disapprovingly. "That thing looks like it came from a garbage can."

"It did." I offered it to him again. "Taste it."

"I'm not eating something from a garbage can. If you want to know what it tastes like, taste it yourself."

"I can't."

From the look I gave him, George must have realized I suspected alcohol was an issue. He knew most of my story. He finished filling the tank on the tractor, then stepped down to the ground and, reluctantly, took the orange from me. He wiped it on his shirt sleeve, then pressed it to his lips and sucked. Almost at once he handed it back to me. "Vodka," he said.

"You're sure?"

"I'm sure. Taste it for yourself if you don't believe me."

"No thanks."

"Then smell it."

"I don't want to do that, either."

"Most people think you can't smell vodka," he said. "But after it evaporates a little you can smell the alcohol, especially as it begins to break down. Where'd that orange come from?"

"The trash can in the shop."

He grimaced. "That's not good."

"Don't say anything just yet."

"You can't let it slide," he said.

"I'm not. I just want to find out more about what's going on before I say anything."

George frowned. "Vodka in an orange. These guys are creative; I'll give them that."

"It's an old trick. Cut a small hole in it to fill it, or use a syringe to inject it, then you can sit around sucking on it and no one will ever suspect anything. Guys used to sneak it into school that way."

After talking to George, I took the orange to the shop and hid it on a shelf, then walked over to the house and met Jessica as she was about to leave. She was by the car when I caught up to her. "I spoke to the priest at St. Francis Church. They have a daycare for babies. Opens at six thirty in the morning. Runs until six thirty at night."

"I can't afford daycare," she said.

"You don't have to. It's all arranged. Just take her there in the morning."

"But I—"

I cut her off. "Just take her there in the morning, okay?"

"Okay."

"They're expecting you."

She opened the car door, then paused. "Did you tell anyone about me?"

"I only told Father Brennan. So he would know to expect you."

"Why are you doing this?"

"She can't stay at home alone," I said. "Someone will find out and report it. Then the state will take her."

She seemed on the verge of tears. "And if Lewis finds out, I'll be fired."

"He won't hear it from me."

She sat behind the steering wheel, and I pushed the door closed. "First thing in the morning," I said.

She started the car, then glanced up at me. "Thank you."

"You're welcome."

Since seeing some of the guys in the field with the pickup truck, playing when they were supposed to be working, I had been curious about what they did when they thought no one was watching. Seeing Norm with that vodka orange told me that whatever they were doing probably wasn't good. They were a clever bunch, but I was confident it wouldn't be difficult to catch them in the act.

Late that night, I drove to a spot on the dirt road near the entrance to the farm and parked the truck behind a clump of bushes. In an hour or two, I heard the sound of an approaching vehicle. I slid low in the seat to avoid being seen and watched through the windshield. When the vehicle appeared, I recognized it as one of the farm's pickups and as it passed by, I saw Dillon, Gary, and Rick seated inside. Dillon was driving. I listened for the sound of the engine as they continued down the road and when they were far enough away, I drove from my hiding place and followed them with my headlights off.

At the highway, they turned left and started toward Alexandria. I did, too, and stayed behind them all the way to the north side of town. They parked around the corner from a bar and started up the sidewalk, laughing and joking with each other. I parked one block behind them, then walked to their truck and waited at the rear bumper.

In a little while, Dillon, Gary, and Rick returned, laughing and joking as before. I heard them before I saw them. Gary and Rick seemed to be drunk. When they were almost to the truck, I stepped out from the back and waited, my arms folded across my chest. It took them a moment to see me and another to recognize me, but when they did, their mouths dropped open in a look of horror. I stared at them a moment, then turned aside and walked away.

The next morning, I was waiting for Lewis when he arrived at his office in the barn. "We have a problem," I said, and I set the orange from the day before on his desk.

He stared at it a moment, then asked, "Is something wrong with it?"

"Norm was sucking on it yesterday."

"And?" He seemed unconcerned.

"It had been filled with vodka."

He snatched up the orange and sniffed it, then scowled. "It was filled with something, that's for sure. How do you know it's vodka?"

"I had George check it yesterday," I explained. "He said it was vodka."

"It was Norm's?"

"Yeah. And that's not all. Three of the guys were out last night."

"Out?" He scowled. "Out of the house?"

"Out of the house and off the farm," I replied."

He frowned. "What are you talking about?"

"Dillon, Gary, and Rick took that old pickup they use in the field and drove it to town."

"Alexandria?"

"Yeah."

Lewis seemed skeptical. "How did they get the keys to it?"

"George sent Alan, Norm, and Rick to work on the fence. He let them use the truck to do it. Rick conveniently forgot to return the keys."

"But if they snuck off in the night, someone would have heard them."

"Not if they pushed the truck out to the road."

"Did you see them do that?"

"No."

Lewis turned away. "Well, without that, I don't see how we can do anything. Probably just a rumor."

He wanted to sweep it all away and pretend nothing ever happened, but I wasn't going to let him do that. "I saw them," I said flatly.

"You saw them?"

"I was pretty sure they were up to something, so I parked up on the dirt road and waited. I saw them come by and followed them."

"Where did they go?"

"To a bar on the north side of town."

"Did you go in there?"

"No," I replied. "I waited for them to come out."

"They saw you?"

"Yeah. I was standing behind the truck and when they came out of the bar, I stepped out in front of them."

"What did you say to them?"

"Nothing."

"What did they say to you?"

"They were speechless."

Lewis picked up the orange and studied it again. "What they won't try," he mused. "Why didn't you come to me first instead of going to George and instead of following them?"

"I knew you wouldn't want to believe they could do something like this, and I knew you would grill me for proof. And you told me I wasn't a group leader, that Doug and Mike would take care of things with the guys, and that I should stick to working in the shop. But I didn't think Doug and Mike would believe me either, so I decided to check it out for myself."

"And they actually took the pickup to town?"

"Drove it to the Blue Tarpon."

Lewis put the orange on his desk and leaned back in his chair. "This is a problem," he said.

"Yeah," I replied. "A big problem."

"It's bigger than you think, though." Lewis opened a desk drawer and took out a letter, then handed it to me. The letter was from a donor and mentioned a twenty-five-thou-sand-dollar check that had been enclosed with it.

I read it and looked over at Lewis. "How is this a prob-lem?"

"The guy who sent that letter, and the check it mentions, is Gary's uncle. He has sent one just like it every month since Gary came here."

"That's a lot of money."

"Tell me about it. For the first time in a long time, we haven't had to worry about which bills to pay first."

I handed him the letter and took a seat. Lewis rested his arms on his lap and closed his eyes. "You're sure Gary was one of them?"

"Yes," I said. "Ask them yourself."

Lewis sighed. "I will."

That afternoon, Frank and Pete worked with me in the shop. When we finished and they were about to leave, I noticed a van parked outside the farmhouse. Mike, one of the group leaders, stood beside it, holding the door open. Frank and Pete noticed it, too, and we watched as Dillon came from the house with a suitcase.

"They're sending him home?" Frank asked.

"I knew they would," Pete said.

"Think they'll send anyone else home?"

Pete stared straight ahead. "Rick's the one they should cut."

By then, most of the other students had arrived from the field and were gathered outside the house. Doug and Mike were outnumbered, and I wasn't sure what would happen next, so I walked up there to see if I could help keep things under control. Frank and Pete followed, and we all watched as Dillon, without comment or gesture, set his suitcase on the second seat of the van and got in beside it. Mike got in on the driver's side.

Everyone watched as the van crested the hill and disappeared. For a while, they stood in silence, staring into the distance as if each one was trying to make sense of what had happened.

Finally, Pete shook his head. "That ain't right."

"Dillon was the driver," someone said, as if that explained it.

"I heard it was all his idea," Ron offered. "That's why they made him leave."

"They should have bounced the others, too."

"I heard they let Gary stay because his folks gave a lot of money."

"Dillon ain't got no money."

"Dillon ain't got nobody."

"Rick had the key to the truck. Why did he get to stay?"

"Okay, guys," Doug said. "Let's go inside and get cleaned up. It's almost time for dinner."

Pete gave him a look. "If my old man gave a bunch of money, would you cut me some slack?"

"They all had the option of staying," Doug explained. "Dillon chose to leave."

"Where's he going? Prison?"

"I don't know."

"Didn't he have a sentence hanging over him?"

"Look—"

Pete interrupted. "You're telling me he chose to go to prison?"

Doug stepped closer. "Listen to me." He tapped Pete on the chest with his finger for emphasis. "The only question you need to worry about is where you're going."

Pete wouldn't give up. "How'd they get out of the house last night, Doug?"

"Watch it," Doug snapped.

"I'm serious," Pete said. "How'd they get out without anyone knowing they were gone?"

"Yeah, Doug," Reuben chided. "That's a good question. We go to the bathroom after lights out; you know about it. Somebody coughs in the dark; you ask about it the next morning. But you never asked about Gary or Dillon or Rick. How'd they get out of the house without you or Mike knowing about it?"

It was a good question and one I'd had myself. Floors in the house creaked at every step. That truck was old and loose and loud. And if they really had pushed it over the hill before starting it, how did they do it? The truck was heavy, and the hill was steeper than it appeared.

Doug glared at Reuben. "You want to join them?"

Reuben frowned. "Join them? Join who? What are you talking about?"

"Hey," Frank said. "Where are they?" He craned his neck, searching. "Anybody seen them this afternoon?"

"Seen who?" Alan asked.

"Gary and Rick."

"Don't worry about them," Doug said, and he gestured toward the door. "Just get inside and get ready for dinner."

There was no major announcement about disciplinary measures against Gary and Rick, but word got around, and I soon learned they spent the daylight hours of the next four weeks in the swamp on the far side of the property, repairing fences and clearing brush from the fencerow. When that task was completed, they were put to work cutting firewood in a stand of trees not too far from the cottage where I lived. I saw them once or twice as they entered the woods at dawn and a few times when they left it just after sunset.

The trouble cast a pall over the farm. Students complied with the program and with the expectations of staff members, but they did it with little of their initiative and no creativity. I continued to engage them in projects at the shop, but they were small in scale and failed to inspire anyone with a genuine interest in discovery, including me.

CHAPTER 11

Summer faded into fall, and everyone was busy harvesting the last of the corn crop, then the peanuts and pecans. I was settling into life at the farm, but I encountered bouts of loneliness at night similar to those I had at the apartment when Julia left me. The cottage. The darkness. The isolation. When it became too much, I sat outside on the porch and let the rural nighttime sounds soothe my soul.

Frank and I continued our routine of attending morning Mass at St. Francis in Alexandria, which was a boost to my emotional well-being. Getting there was stressful at times—everyone was pressed for time with work and school—but I needed it, and I didn't want to convey a wrong message by telling Frank we had to forego Mass for something else. He enjoyed the service and seemed to be growing from the experience. Beginning each day that way kept me stable.

One morning, on the way back to the farm, we passed a sign for the Tioga Speedway. From the condition of the sign, it must have been there all the while with us passing it every day, but I never noticed it until that morning. An arrow on the sign pointed toward a dirt road. I gestured to it as we went by. "Ever been to a speedway?"

"No," Frank replied with a laugh. "They don't have them in the French Quarter, and I'd never been out of the city until I came up here."

At the next intersection, I turned the truck around and, despite being pressed for time, drove back to where we'd seen the sign, then turned onto the dirt road. A little way down the road, we came to a large open field in the middle of which was a racetrack—a dirt oval with bleachers on two sides, a press box atop the closest one, and a concession stand at either end. A sign attached to the bleachers proclaimed, "Fastest Dirt In The South." We drove across the field and circled the outside of the track, looking it over as we idled along.

A truck was parked near one of the concession stands. There was a trailer hitched to it and on the trailer was a clunker of a car someone had pounded into a contraption that looked like a race car, of sorts. I brought my pickup to a stop alongside it and we stared out the window at the car.

"Ever seen anything like that?" I asked.

"Only in a magazine," Frank replied. "My cousin used to be interested in that kind of stuff."

"Looks like a car made specially to run on dirt. Maybe a little bit automobile and a little bit…something else."

Frank laughed. "Kinda heavy on the something else, I'd say."

A man came from the concession stand and made his way toward us. "You interested in buying it?" he asked, gesturing to the car on the trailer.

"Didn't realize you were selling it," I replied.

He pointed to the car and then I noticed a For Sale sign on the back window. "You've actually raced it?" I asked.

He seemed proud. "Won the Late Model Modified championship with it last year."

"With that?" I pointed to the car.

"Yeah," he said. "With that. Don't look like much on the outside, but it'll fly." He reached over and patted the fender of the car with his hand. "Season won't start until summer, but you better get it now while you can. Come spring, somebody else will own it."

I was intrigued. "They race that kind of car here at this track?"

"Yeah," he said. "This place was full of them last year."

"I'd like to see that. Are they having races?"

"Nah," he replied. "Track won't open again until the first weekend in June." He gestured over his shoulder toward the concession stand. "They can tell you all about it in there."

I parked the truck by the concession stand and Frank followed me inside to an office in the back where a lady was seated at a desk. When she learned why we were there, she was all too glad to fill us in on the details of racing. Half an hour later, we returned to the truck with a rule book that covered the three classes of cars that competed at the track.

Frank leafed through it, but he was skeptical. "Are you gonna start racing?"

"Nope," I replied with a grin. "We're gonna start racing."

"We?" Frank's eyes were wide. "As in you and me?"

"As in you, me, and everyone in the group."

He laughed. "Racing might be popular up here but in case you've forgotten, most of us are from New Orleans. We're drug addicts and alcoholics, not rednecks and street racers."

"You don't think the guys in the group will be interested in it?"

"There aren't three people in the group who even have a driver's license."

My grin widened. "Sounds perfect." And it really did. Something none of us knew anything about, including me. We could learn about it together.

Frank shook his head. "We gotta work the farm," he said. "They'll have two hundred acres of potatoes to dig in the spring. We won't have time to work on a race car."

"We'll have all winter," I replied. "And we'll be finished with the potatoes by June. I think we'll have plenty of time to get a race car ready and get the farm work done, too."

At noon, while everyone else ate lunch, I read the race-track rule book. The track sponsored competition in three classes—Modifieds, Late Models, and Bombers. Modifieds were the fastest and most sophisticated, with unlimited horsepower and very few restrictions. They resembled production automobiles, but not by much. Late Models were a slower version of the Modifieds with more restrictions and fewer options in how the engine could be configured. There were also limitations on modifications to the original car body. Cars in that class were more like sedans in the parking lot, except for the engine.

The Bombers were the simplest class—strictly stock automobiles and engines with modifications limited to only production parts from the manufacturer of the car. Chevrolet car bodies, for instance, required a Chevrolet engine prepared using only original Chevrolet parts. Aftermarket add-ons weren't allowed. From pictures I'd seen in the office, Bombers were little more than worn-out street cars with roll bars and slightly wider tires included for safety. It was a class of racing well suited for our guys. All we needed was a car.

From what I had observed and encountered at the farm, I was certain that if I asked for permission to build a race car of any kind, Lewis would turn me down without seriously considering it. But I was equally certain this was the perfect project for our guys. One through which we could teach them a broad range of subjects—math, physics, basic engine technology, tool usage—all the things Lewis said he wanted the students to learn—in a context that gave it purpose, meaning, and significance.

Cars, speed, competition, and a bunch of guys—what could possibly go wrong? But to do it, we had to have a car. Not necessarily a functioning car. In fact, it would be better if it were not in very good condition at all. For a moment, that part had me stumped…and then I thought of George, the farm manager. He knew everyone who lived within a hundred miles of the farm. If anyone could solve my dilemma about a car, he could.

While the others finished eating lunch, I found George sitting on a five-gallon bucket in the shade by the barn, near the concrete pad where we washed equipment. He listened while I told him my idea, then gave me one of those looks. "You think racing is the answer for what's wrong with these guys?"

"I think it'll help," I said.

He shook his head. "Lewis will never go for it."

"Maybe," I responded. "But at least we could build the car. And working on it will give the guys something to do that they've never thought of before. If we can't race it, we can always sell it."

George grinned. "Sell it?"

"Yeah."

"You think they sell that kind of thing?"

"A guy at the track tried to sell me one this morning."

"You were at the racetrack?"

"The one in Tioga," I replied.

"I haven't been there in years." George scratched his

chin thoughtfully, then said, "I got a friend who might be able to help. I'll ask him."

A few days later, a tow truck arrived at the farm with a dilapidated 1967 Chevy Chevelle hooked on the back. The car was rusted, dented, and coated with dirt and grime. Kudzu vines dangled from the roof posts and a clump of weeds hung off the rear bumper.

The tow truck driver dropped the car near the concrete wash pad. When he had it in place and was ready to leave, he turned to me. "They told me I was supposed to get a receipt for this. Something about a donation."

Pete walked to a cabinet just inside the barn and returned with a preprinted form that he handed to me. "I've seen them use these before."

I filled in the blank spaces on the form with the information that seemed relevant, scribbled my signature at the bottom, and handed it to the driver. "Will that do?"

"I'm sure it will." He stuffed it into his pocket without reading it, climbed into the cab of the tow truck, and drove away.

As the truck disappeared, the guys gathered around the car. "What are we doing with that?" Rick asked.

I stood near the rear bumper of the car. "Does anybody know what this is?"

"Junk," someone replied.

"A wreck."

"A rusted worthless wreck," another added.

Their comments made me grin. "This, gentlemen," I announced, "is a race car."

They howled with laughter. "A race car?"

"A race car," I said calmly.

Pete shook his head. "Are you out of your mind?"

"Even if it is a race car," Reuben said, "what are we going to do with it?"

"Drive it," I responded.

Reuben looked askance. "Drive it?"

"Drive it or sell it," I said. "But first, we have to work on it."

They groaned. "What kind of work?"

"Is this more of that make-the-farm-better crap?"

I ignored the comments and pointed to the fencerow. "Down there a little way you'll find some steel pipe. About as big around as your arm. It's lying in the weeds. Go find it and start dragging it up here."

"What for?"

"You'll see later," I said.

Just then, Lewis appeared. He stood with his hands on his hips and stared at the car. "What are you doing with this junker?"

"We're making a race car," I replied confidently.

Lewis frowned. "A race car?"

"Yeah," I said. "A race car."

He stared a little longer, then gestured for me to follow and we walked to the front of the barn. When we were out of sight of the others, he turned to me with a glare. "Are you out of your mind? The last thing we need is to get these guys excited about something as ridiculous as racing."

"What we're doing with them isn't working," I replied. It was a bold statement, but one I was certain was true.

The words seemed to hit him hard, but I think he knew I was right. "What we're doing is working just fine." He said it with a sharp tone, but his heart wasn't in it.

"Three guys took a joy ride into town for a night of drinking," I responded. "One of them chose to go home to who knows what rather than stay here and accept the consequences. The others think they're nothing but free farm labor. And you think we're doing fine?"

Lewis sighed. "Ok. We might have problems, and I'm not sure what to do about it, but I know one thing. These men aren't going racing. They're going to the field."

He walked away and before I could go after him, Doug appeared. "All right, men. Party's over. Let's get to the field."

A collective groan went up. "I knew it wouldn't happen," Ron groused. "Soon as we get excited about something, they put an end to it."

"Leave it to Doug to squelch our interests."

"Toting water for the boss."

Rather than defend Doug, I hurried to catch up with Lewis. "Why did you do that?"

"These men are drug addicts," he said. "They've lived in a dream world most of their lives. They don't need another dream. They need to face up to reality. Besides, we don't have the money for a race car or any other dream."

"Everyone needs a dream," I argued. "That's what motivates us to get up in the morning." Lewis didn't respond. I kept going. "What if it doesn't cost the farm anything?"

"Like that'll actually happen."

"No," I said. "Seriously. What if it doesn't cost the farm anything?"

He turned to face me. "If you want to teach them how to work on cars, that's fine. But you have to find a way to pay for it. And don't put stupid ideas in their heads. They have enough of those as it is."

That evening, I rode into Alexandria to a bookstore and bought a couple of magazines and a book about automobile racing. I thought if we were going to build a race car, I should familiarize myself with the sport. I knew how to repair automobiles, but, like Frank, I had never attended a race, much less driven in one.

When I returned, I found Jessica's car parked at the cottage. She was sitting on the front porch with her baby in a car seat on the floor next to her. I parked the truck and walked over to her.

"Thanks for helping with daycare." She smiled and rocked the baby gently. "I took her there the next morning. Everyone was very nice to us."

"Good."

"Yeah." She nodded. "It's a great place."

"What did your boyfriend think of it?"

She looked away. "He's gone."

I'd never met the guy, but I was glad to hear he had moved on. "Where did he go?"

"I don't know." She shrugged. "He was staying out all night and only going to class once in a while. And he didn't work."

"That's not good."

"I got tired of it, so I told him to leave."

I wasn't sure what else to say but she didn't seem interested in leaving so I said, "You want to come inside?"

"Sure."

She picked up the baby and I held the door for her. They sat on the couch with the baby beside her. I offered her a soft drink and took a seat in a chair that gave me a view of the couch and the window that looked onto the pasture.

We talked for a while, but it was awkward, and I wondered if she had been hoping for something romantic between us. She was attractive and at another time in my life I might have been interested, but she was young. Not young enough to be my daughter but young enough that the age difference mattered, so I avoided showing any hint of inclination in that direction. But it was a strange moment and I wondered why she was there, if not for that.

A few minutes later, I heard footsteps on the porch and glanced out the window but saw no one. I opened the door and checked to be sure. When I came back inside, she was sitting on the edge of the sofa, looking expectantly in my direction. "See anyone?" she asked.

"No," I replied.

"Might have been him," she said.

"Who?"

"My boyfriend."

"Ex-boyfriend," I corrected.

"Yeah."

"You think he followed you out here?"

"Wouldn't put it past him."

The whole thing made me uneasy—her being there, with the baby, and now the ex-boyfriend knowing where the cottage was located. I was about to tell her to leave but the baby started to fuss, and she decided on her own that it was time to go. I walked with her to the car and as she drove away, I heard a truck engine start, but I never saw it.

Later that night, as I prepared for bed, I propped a straight-back chair against the front door and wedged it against the doorknob. I did the same for the back door and, as an added measure, placed a few pieces of flatware in a metal pot and set it in the hall, thinking an intruder might hit it and awaken me.

Much to my relief, the night passed without further incident, and I awakened to a cool, crisp morning. After breakfast at the cottage, I went to the shop and was waiting when the students arrived for our morning session. I had moved the car to the concrete wash pad and gathered the guys around it.

"Before we can—"

Norm interrupted. "Are we really gonna build a race car?"

"We are really building a race car," I replied. "But before we can—"

"Are you gonna let us drive it?" someone asked.

"Yes," I said, and I meant it, even if they only drove it up and down the dirt road.

"But what about racing?" Rick said. "Are we going to drive it in a race?"

"We'll have to work out the details of that when we get to it."

"There you go," Pete said with a dejected tone. "It's this

way, but it may be something else. We've heard that more times than we can count."

"I haven't worked all of the details out yet," I explained. For some reason, I glanced to the left and caught sight of the pasture. "But I'll tell you this, if we can get the car built and running, we'll take it to the pasture, and you can all take turns driving it there."

"All of us?" Rick asked.

"All of you. But before we can do that, we have to build a car. And before we can build anything out of this car," I said, patting a fender for emphasis, "what do we have to do?" When no one answered, I asked again. "Where does every job like this begin?"

"We clean it," Frank said.

"That's right," I said. "We have to get it cleaned up." The power washer was by the car, and I gestured to it. "Who wants to run the washer first?" When no one responded, I handed the hose to Pete.

"I did it last time," he protested. "With that potato thing."

"Good," I replied. "You have experience. You can show Rick how it's done, and he can go next."

"I had a turn on that digger thing, too," Rick said. "That's enough for me."

I connected a water hose to the washer, then walked over to the faucet and turned on the water. Reuben started the engine, and a reluctant Pete began cleaning the car. Rick tried to slip away, but I caught him and brought him back.

"If you want to drive the car, you have to do the work."

"It's too cool to play with water," he protested.

"Get busy," I said. "Everyone gets a turn, just like before."

A few minutes later, Mike arrived. "Lewis wants to see you," he said. The tone of his voice was serious.

"What about?" I asked.

"I don't know, but I think he meant for you to come now."

Lewis was seated at his desk when I arrived at the office. "You wanted to see me?"

"Yeah," he said. "Someone saw Jessica at your cabin last night. What was that about?"

"She came by," I replied. "I didn't invite her."

"What you do with your own time is your business," he said. "But I understand she has a baby." A smile came and went as he said it.

"Yes. She does." I wasn't sure what he meant by that, but I avoided a more pointed response.

He raised an eyebrow. "Is it yours?" And again, he seemed to smile, but only for an instant.

"No," I replied.

"Are you sure?"

"Yes, I'm sure." My voice was a little more strident than I intended, but the question aggravated me. "Why are you asking me this? You know it's impossible. I didn't know her before you introduced us, and I've only been here a few months."

"You sure about that? You could have gotten her pregnant before you arrived and took this job to be near her."

The suggestion was ridiculous and made me angry. "And I could have come here with a secret plan to turn the farm into a distillery," I argued, "and steal the corn crop to make moonshine, but I didn't. I'm just Jake from New Orleans, who came here because Father Deasy said it was a good opportunity. But how do you know she was at my house?"

Lewis looked away. "I can't say."

I stared at him a moment, thinking, then I remembered the truck I'd heard. "Last night. Someone was on the porch. They told you."

"I can't say."

"There are only three people who know that I know she has a child. Jessica, Frank, and me, so—"

"Frank?" he asked, interrupting. "One of the students knows, and you knew, and I didn't?"

Then I realized the real problem—he wasn't the first to find out. "Frank was in the barn when she told me about her."

"Her?"

"The child is a girl," I explained. "But you didn't learn this from Frank. He wouldn't talk to you about her. And you didn't learn this from me. You only heard about the baby from someone else." I had a knowing smile. "You heard this from Mike or Doug."

Lewis looked away again. "I'm not saying." His expression told me I was right.

The sound of an automobile drifted through from outside. I recognized the engine noise as Jessica's. "I think Jessica just arrived," I said, gesturing over my shoulder. "Ask her yourself."

"I will," he said. "I asked her to join us."

In a few minutes, Jessica came to the office, and Lewis asked her about her visit to the cabin. "I just needed to get out," she said.

"I understand you have a baby."

She shot an accusing look in my direction, but I waved her off. "He didn't hear it from me."

She turned back to Lewis. "Why are you asking about this?"

"Is Jake the father?"

"No," she said indignantly. "He's not the father. And why do you care if he is? It's none of your business."

"You were seen at Jake's house last night," Lewis said. "I wanted to make sure he wasn't the father."

Jessica was angry. "What difference does it make if he is or isn't?"

"Truthfulness," Lewis replied.

"You think I'm lying?"

Lewis wasn't angry, but he was determined to get an answer. "I think you've been coming here, working with the guys, under the assumption that you're a college student working on a teaching degree. Now I find out about a baby and a visit to Jake's cottage, and I want to know what's going on."

Jessica took a deep breath. "Look," she said, "the father is a guy from Lafayette. He was supposed to be going to school while I paid the bills, then he would work and I would go to school. But I found out he'd been partying with someone else instead of going to class, so I threw him out. When Jake found I had a baby, he found a daycare that would take care of Amie."

"Amie. That's the baby's name?"

"Yes," she said. "I came by last night to thank him for helping me."

Lewis seemed to understand. "So, you aren't in school now?"

"I had to work to pay the bills and support my daughter."

"You had wanted to be a teacher?"

"Yes," Jessica said. "And I still do. That's why I like working here."

"Okay," Lewis said. "That's all I wanted to ask about."

"Do I still have a job?" Jessica asked.

"Sure," Lewis replied.

"Good." And Jessica left the room.

When she was gone, Lewis looked over at me. "You found a daycare for her baby?"

"Yes."

He had a quizzical expression. "And the baby's not yours?"

"No," I replied. "You heard what she said."

"Why did you do that?"

"She needed help. I could help her. So, I did."

"How much does the daycare cost?"

I didn't want to tell him, but I didn't think I could refuse. "Fifty dollars a week," I said.

"Where is it?"

"St. Francis."

"The church?"

"Yes."

Lewis straightened himself and scooted closer to the desk. "Have Father Brennan send me the bill."

After talking to Lewis, I went to find Mike. The information about Jessica had to come from someone who worked with her, and he seemed the most likely candidate. I found him in the tractor shed. "Which one of you went to Lewis about Jessica?"

He avoided my gaze. "What do you mean?"

"You know exactly what I mean." I moved in front of him. "I found out she has a baby and was having trouble juggling childcare and work and tried to help. For some unknown reason, you went to Lewis and made up a story about me being the father. Why did you do that?"

"That wasn't me," he said.

"Then who was it?"

He looked up at me. "Doug," he said.

The answer confirmed my suspicion, but it astounded me, too. "Why did he do that? Why would he lie to Lewis about something like that?"

Mike had a knowing look that suggested to me that Doug was involved with her.

"Nah," I said, shaking my head. "He's not the father."

"I don't think so, either."

But there was more to it than that. "What are you not telling me?" I asked.

Mike stopped what he was doing and focused on the conversation. "When she started working here, we both liked her," he explained. "Only it was different with Doug. I liked being around her and talking to her. Doug was obsessed with the idea of having sex with her."

"Sex?" I frowned. "He's a counselor in a rehab program run by the church."

"That doesn't guarantee anything about a person's character."

"It ought to." And I really believed that, even though I had my own shortcomings.

"Perhaps it should," he said. "I'm just saying, he was obsessed with her."

"Why was he so fixated on her?"

Mike shrugged. "That's just Doug. All he could talk about was how she already had a baby and knew what it was like to be in bed with someone and he was sure she wouldn't turn him down."

"So, he made a pass at her?"

"Several," Mike replied.

"And she turned him down."

Mike nodded. "And he got mad about it. When he heard what you did with fixing the car and finding a daycare, he was livid."

"At me?"

"Yes."

"Why?" It seemed impossible to me that someone in his position could be so small-minded and petty.

"He felt challenged by you and betrayed by her," Mike said. "He wanted to ruin you both. I don't know how he found out she was at your house, but that's why he went over there."

"He was the one on the porch."

"Yes."

I shook my head. "What an idiot."

"That's about the sum of it," he agreed.

"Where is he?"

"I don't know," Mike replied. "He left the house this morning, and I haven't seen him since."

After talking to Mike, I went to find Jessica. She was sitting at the dining room table in the house. "That was a strange conversation," she said as I entered the room.

"Yes," I replied, "it was."

"How did he find out about the baby and daycare and me coming to your house?"

"Doug told him."

She scowled. "He's a pervert."

"What last name does your baby have?"

"Doucette. Why?"

"Does Doug know who the father is?"

"No. Why?"

"He doesn't know the guy's name?"

"No," she said. "Why?"

"I haven't seen him and I'm wondering where he is and what he's up to."

She looked concerned. "You think he'll cause trouble?"

"I wouldn't put anything past him. Where is Amie?"

"At the daycare. I don't think they would let anything happen to her."

"Maybe we should call them just to be sure."

"I don't think he'll be a problem. He's not that ambitious or concerned."

We were silent for a moment, then she said, "I saw you going over to that shed a while ago. Did you talk to Mike?"

"Yes."

Her countenance darkened. "He told you about Doug?"

I was unsure of how much to say. "He told me how Doug felt about you."

"It was more than just that," she said. "He came to my apartment two or three times."

"I thought your boyfriend was living there."

"He was, but Doug came while he was in class." She paused to correct herself. "While he was supposed to be in class."

"What happened?"

"Doug got pretty rough," she said.

I was horrified. "Did he rape you?"

"No. It didn't get that far. But he was rather forceful."

"Don't minimize it," I said. "If he did something to you, you need to tell somebody."

She pulled up her sleeve to reveal a bruise in the shape of a handprint.

My jaw went slack at the sight of it. "He did that?"

She nodded in response.

"Why?"

"He came to see me last week," she said. "This is what he left." She ran her finger lightly over the bruise.

I took her gently by the hand and tugged at her to get up. "Come on," I said.

She stood. "What are you doing?"

"We're going to see Lewis," I said. She didn't resist.

As we came from the house and started toward the barn, Pete shouted to me. "Are we doing anything else this morning?"

"Wash the car with a rag," I said. "And use soap." It was the first thing I could think of. "Get it clean, inside and out."

Pete said something in response, but I ignored him and kept moving toward the barn, taking Jessica with me. We found Lewis still at his desk. I closed the door behind us and gestured to Jessica. "Show him your arm."

She pulled up her sleeve. Lewis stood and leaned forward for a closer look. "How did this happen?"

Jessica hesitated. I gave her a nudge. "Tell him what happened."

"Doug came to my apartment."

Lewis collapsed in his chair as Jessica told him the details. I made sure she included all of Doug's visits.

CHAPTER 13

The next day, when the students came to the shop for the morning session, I divided them into groups and put them to work gutting the car. None of the standard interior components were necessary. One group removed the door panels. Another the seats, carpet, wiring, and headliner. A third group removed the hood and disconnected the engine in preparation for removing it from the car. We needed it out of the car so we could disassemble it and determine if it was usable. I hoped it would be. Finding a different engine would pose a problem for us that I wasn't sure we could overcome.

Frank, working with Rick on the interior, seemed to enjoy his assigned task the most. Pete, helping Reuben with the engine, did not. "This is a waste of time," he complained. "I'm not working on cars for a living. And I'm a mess." His clothes really were dirty.

Don, who was also helping with the engine, added, "Isn't racing for rednecks?"

"Go fast, turn left," Frank answered from inside the car. "You don't have to be a redneck to do that."

"If you build the car," I said, by way of reminder, "you get to drive the car."

They stopped complaining, but I could tell Pete wasn't satisfied. I wasn't sure he would ever be satisfied with anything.

Despite their lack of enthusiasm, by the time their morning in the shop came to a close, the interior of the car had been stripped of the seats, the dash, and the roof liner. The windows and roll-up mechanisms had been removed from the doors, and most of the parts had been stacked inside the shop with the smaller pieces in boxes. The engine had been disconnected from everything except the mounting brackets and the transmission and was almost ready for removal.

As they cleaned up in preparation for class with Jessica, I glanced out the shop door and saw Doug coming from the farmhouse. His car was parked near the steps, and I watched as he loaded it with what appeared to be his personal belongings—a suitcase, several cardboard boxes, and a couple of plastic bags. Lewis stood on the porch with Mike. As Doug came from the house, they inspected each item before it went into the trunk of the car.

Rick was beside me. "What's going on with that?" he asked, gesturing toward the house.

"Looks like Doug is leaving," I replied.

"Why?"

I felt certain Doug had been fired for the way he treated Jessica, but I didn't want to be the one to explain it to the group.

Gary joined us. "Is this about last night?"

"What happened?" I asked.

"He and Mike were arguing about something," he said. "I don't know what it was, but it was pretty loud."

"Yeah," Palmer, who had also joined us, added. "They were shouting. And I mean really shouting."

"They really were loud," Rick said, nodding in agreement.

Doug came from the house again, this time empty-handed. It was obvious from his body language that he was angry. Mike tried to say something to him, but Doug shrugged him off and got into the car, then drove away.

A few minutes later, Lewis came to the shop. "I guess you saw Doug leaving." He spoke to me, but the guys were standing with us.

"Yeah," I said. "Is he gone for good?"

"Yes."

Rick glanced over at us. "Why did he leave?"

"He had some personal trouble," Lewis replied.

Rick frowned. "Personal trouble?"

I smiled at him. "The kind that's better if we don't discuss it."

Rick looked embarrassed. I put my hand on his shoulder in a reassuring gesture. "It's okay," I said. "I like your curiosity."

"Doug was a good guy," Rick said. "But he hasn't been himself lately."

Lewis turned back to me. "With him gone, Mike will need some help with the guys until we find a replacement."

"Who are you gonna get to do that?" I asked.

"You," Lewis said, pointing to me.

"Ha!" The comment caught me off-guard. "You said I wasn't a group leader."

"You are now," Lewis said. "At least until we get someone else."

Being a group leader would have suited me fine when I arrived at the farm. Now, with the car and a project I thought had the potential to engage the guys, running the group on a daily basis seemed like a distraction.

"Mike can handle things at night," Lewis continued. "You and he can work out the routine for what you do during the day. Just make sure the schedule is covered."

"Okay," I replied, but I wasn't enthusiastic.

"And just so you know," Lewis added, "I talked to the dean at the university. Jessica can return for the fall semester. All she has to do is notify the registrar. She won't have to reapply and go through that process."

"Good," I said.

"They've arranged to give her a grant that will cover the cost of tuition and books."

That was great, but she still needed a place to stay. "What about a place to live?" I asked.

"I have a friend who lives near the campus. He has a garage apartment. He'll let her live in it for free as long as she goes to class and continues to work for us."

"And the baby?"

"A church near the school has a daycare program. My wife knows the preacher's wife. They'll let her come for free."

"So, she'll continue coming here as usual?" For some reason that seemed important. She was too young for me. I was too old for her. But I liked her and wanted the best for her.

"Yeah." He nodded. "That's part of the deal. Go to class, teach here, quit whatever second or third job she had in Alexandria."

Lewis had arranged to put Jessica's life back together. I was glad he did, but I couldn't help feeling like this was a way to placate her and keep her from causing trouble over what happened. Doug was the farm's employee. Jessica was, too. Lewis had been unaware of what transpired between them because he had neglected to supervise either of them. Even back then—in the 1980s—a lawyer could have easily made a court case out of it against the farm, the church, and whoever else sponsored the program. I had the sense Lewis knew that and was trying to steer everyone away from a bad result.

"Thanks for helping her," I said.

"Glad to do it."

As he walked away, Frank said. "I've been thinking about college, too."

I forgot he'd been standing there the whole time. "What about it?" I asked.

"When I get finished here, I think I might go to LSU. Do

you think I could do that?"

"I think you can do anything you decide to do. But if you want to attend LSU, you have to get your GED first."

"I can do that," he said, and he started toward the house for class.

As he walked away, I looked over at Pete. "What about you? What are you really interested in? I know it's not working on cars."

"Cooking," he said quietly.

My eyes were wide with surprise. "Really?" He'd never mentioned an interest in it before.

"Yeah," he said. "I've always enjoyed it."

"They have schools for that in New Orleans."

"I was thinking maybe I should just get a job in a kitchen somewhere," he said. "Work my way up."

"Some people do that," I replied. "Or you could go to school and work in a kitchen at the same time."

Pete winced. "Seems like a lot of work."

"It is," I agreed, "but if you go to school and get a degree, you can get a job as a chef, not just as kitchen help. The school I attended has cooking programs."

"Maybe I'll check into it."

That was the first indication Pete had given that he might be interested in his future. I made a mental note to see if Howard would let him help with meals at the house.

With Doug gone, Mike and I worked out a plan to divide the group responsibilities between us. I already had the students for most of the morning but agreed to help with Jessica's class and lunch. In the afternoon, we split the guys on a rotating basis, half coming to me at the shop one afternoon, the other half the next. And I agreed to remain at the house through dinner before returning to the cottage.

At first, I thought the changes in our routine would disrupt work on the car, but I quickly realized it only made things better. With more guys in the afternoon, we were able to do more work. Within days, we had the engine out of the car, washed, and mounted on an engine stand in the shop.

"This stand," I explained, "will hold the engine and allow us to turn it upside down." I released a brake on the frame of the stand and showed them how it rotated.

"What will we do with it now?" Rick asked.

"Take it apart," I replied.

"How will we get it back together?"

"For now," I said, "we will lay the parts in order on the workbench."

Over the next few days, as the students took apart the engine, I did my best to explain to them how the parts operated together, but with only one engine the class didn't move fast enough to keep them interested. We needed a second engine, and a stand to hold it. As had become my practice, I asked George about it.

"There's an old truck in the back corner of the pasture."

"Does it have an engine in it?"

"I don't know."

"Think anyone would mind if I brought it up here to the shop?"

"It's been there as long as I've been here," he said. "I don't think anyone else even knows it's there."

"What about an engine stand?" I asked with a smile. "Think you could fabricate something like that?"

He grinned. "Let me think about it. I'm sure we can come up with something."

The next day, I took some of the guys and a tractor to the pasture and we pulled the truck to the shop. After they removed the engine and cleaned it, we mounted it to an engine stand that George and some of the guys fabricated from scrap iron. It wasn't as slick as the stand we used with the first engine, but it was sturdy, and I was glad to have it.

In the mornings, when all the students were in the shop together, part of them worked on the engine from the car while the rest worked on the one from the truck. I moved between the two, asking questions about what they were doing and lecturing about how the engines operated. To help with that, I brought a chalkboard into the shop—the old kind we used in school when I attended, with the board affixed to a frame that had casters on the legs so it could be moved around. I used it to draw diagrams of the parts and illustrate their roles in the engine's operation. They were crude drawings, but they served their purpose.

We started at the top, with the carburetor, then worked our way down until we came to the valves and camshaft. After we'd removed the shaft from the first engine and wiped it off, I held it up from them to see. "We've been over the basic function of an engine," I began.

"A thousand times," Ron groaned.

"But now we have to discuss the details," I continued. "Does anyone know what this does?" I gestured with the shaft for emphasis.

Frank spoke up, "Why do they call it a shaft? It's not straight."

The shaft really was straight—the centerline ran down the middle from one end to the other—but it had lobes that rose above the centerline at specific intervals, giving it an uneven appearance. I didn't argue the point. No one was ready for that much complication. Not yet.

"Shaft is a general term," I replied. "It's a part in a machine that turns round and round. It uses that circular motion to transmit power to other parts of the machine. Any idea how this shaft does that or where it's transmitting the power to?"

No one answered, so I explained. "This camshaft turns round and round. As it does, the lobes push up on the ends of the valve stems." I gestured in an attempt to illustrate the point. "That upward push opens the valves and lets gas into the cylinder on one rotation, then comes back around to let the exhaust fumes out on the next. Look at the end of it.

What do you see?" I turned the end of the shaft toward them.

"A round piece of metal," Ron said.

"That's right. Viewed from the end, you can see the shaft is round. Which means, from that perspective, it's a circle. How many degrees are there in a circle?"

They all had a puzzled look. "Come on, guys," I urged. "Somebody knows the answer."

When they didn't respond, I set the shaft on the bench and drew a circle on the chalkboard. "How many degrees are there in a circle?" I asked.

"Three hundred sixty," Pete replied.

"Right. There are three hundred sixty degrees in a circle. The camshaft rotates three hundred sixty degrees for each complete turn. As the lobes come around, they push against the valve stems and hold the valves open." I took a valve from the bench and held it in position against a lobe of the shaft so they could see. It was too cumbersome to manage, so I had Gary hold the valve while I slowly rotated the shaft, making the movement of the lobes obvious. "The length of the lobe at the base and the height of its peak at the top determine how long the valve stays open."

"That wouldn't be very long in an engine," Reuben observed. "Don't the parts move fast even when it's idling?"

"Yes," I said. "The internal parts move too fast to count by looking at them. And too fast to time with a watch. That's one reason why cams are classified by the number of degrees they rotate while holding the valves open. Twenty degrees.

Thirty degrees. You'll hear someone talk about 'degrees of lift.' They're talking about how many degrees the camshaft turns while holding the valves open. It's also known as the camshaft's duration. The total amount of lift provided by a shaft's lobes."

That was more than they wanted to know about camshafts, lobes, and valves, but I gave it to them anyway, knowing I would have to repeat the exercise many times before it became natural to them. I didn't care if they became master mechanics. I just wanted them to have the joy of figuring something out and understanding what it meant.

Work continued on the engines and in a week or two, both were disassembled, and the parts were cleaned. Rather than reassembling both, however, we concentrated on the engine that came from the car and made sure it would actually operate. We rotated the crank and pistons through several cycles, checked the alignment of the pistons with the camshaft, tested cylinder compression, and installed a new ignition system, then pronounced it ready to run. The guys beamed. I was so proud I nearly cried.

As work on the engine neared completion, we brought the car into the shop. When we had it in place, I said, "If we're building a race car, we need to do more than fix the engine."

Everyone looked surprised. "Race car," Rick said. "Is that really what we're building?"

"I told you that from the beginning," I replied.

"I thought you were kidding."

"I did, too," Reuben added.

"Well, I didn't," Frank said proudly.

"If you're on the track," I said, "and you hit another car, or they hit you, you'll want to have something between you and them other than the sheet metal of the car's exterior. That something is called a roll cage."

Pete frowned. "A what cage?"

"A roll cage," I replied. "That's what they call the network of reinforcing bars that go inside the car. It keeps the driver from being crushed if the car rolls over or gets hit."

"The cars hit each other?" Palmer asked.

"Not on purpose, but it happens."

"And we're going to build one of these cages?"

"Do you remember the pipe you brought out of the fencerow?"

Several nodded in response.

"Drag it over to the—"

"Let me guess," Pete said, interrupting. "You want us to clean it."

"Yes." I grinned. "I want you to clean it and set it in the sun so it will dry."

Over the next several weeks, we bent steel pipe into various configurations and cut it to fit across the front of the car, then down both sides between the engine compartment and the rear wheels, and around the gas tank at the rear. Doing that became a project in itself. One that required lots of measuring, drawing, and planning, all of which proved extremely frustrating to everyone and extremely helpful in sharpening their math skills. I recruited George to help weld it all together in a seamless system.

When we finished with the roll cage, we prepared the engine compartment for the engine. George helped us reinforce the frame rails and engine mounts and fabricated sheet metal for the dashboard inside the car. He also helped the guys wire the engine and connect it to a series of gauges that showed water temperature, oil pressure, electrical output from the alternator, and speed of the engine in revolutions per minute. One of George's friends gave us a driver's seat and safety harness, and we installed that, too.

When we were finished, I realized the car still had street tires. That wouldn't work for the track, but we weren't there yet, so I decided to keep quiet about it. We pushed the car from the shop, and Reuben climbed in through the window—the doors had been welded in place with solid seams. He smiled at us through the window.

"See if it'll start," I said.

His eyes opened wide. "Really?"

"Yeah. Really."

He flipped a switch on the dash and pressed a button near the steering column. The engine turned over but failed to start. He looked deflated. Everyone groaned.

"Try it again," I urged.

He repeated the procedure, and still the engine wouldn't start. George came from the barn with a can of ether, a highly combustible gas in aerosol form. It was often used to help start reluctant engines, especially after work had drained the fuel system, which was the case with ours.

"Try this," George said, and he sprayed a shot of ether into the carburetor as Reuben pressed the starter button. The engine coughed and spit and sputtered but kept running, though rough at first. As the temperature came up to normal, the idle improved. I adjusted the settings on the carburetor and before long, the engine ran smoothly.

Reuben was still seated at the steering wheel. I looked in his direction. "Take it once around the barn."

His mouth dropped open. "You want me to drive the car?"

"Yes."

"Around the barn?"

"Yes."

"I've never driven a car before."

I frowned. "You've never driven before?"

"No," he said, shaking his head.

"Well, there's a first time for everything. Go slow and try not to hit anything."

I leaned through the window and helped him put the car in reverse. When he was far enough away from the building,

I showed him how to put it in first gear. As I stepped away, he let out the clutch, and the car started forward.

After Reuben made a lap, everyone else took a turn and when they all had gone once around the building, we drove the car to the pasture. Everyone took a turn there, too. Pete went last, and being over-eager and over-confident, he went too fast. When he attempted to turn the car to start back in our direction, it rolled onto its side. We ran to see about him, but by the time we got there, he was out of the car and laughing.

With everyone helping, we righted the car and used a tractor to pull it back to the barn. Lewis was waiting when we arrived. I knew by the scowl on his face that he was unhappy. "What were you thinking?" he demanded.

"We were just having fun," I said.

"You have to stop this," he insisted. "You're going to get someone killed."

"We can't stop." I gestured to the guys. "Look at them."

They were more excited and happier than they'd been since I arrived. Laughing and howling, they gathered at the rear bumper of the car and, with Reuben at the steering wheel, pushed it to the wash pad. Rick came from the shop with the power washer, Palmer attached the hose, and without a word of complaint they began cleaning the car.

I pointed in their direction. "They've worked harder and more diligently on this car than on anything else since I've been here."

"But this idea of racing," Lewis said. "It's just a dream."

"It's more than just a dream. It's the program you want. It's the program we all want."

He frowned. "What do you mean?"

"It's working just like we wanted," I said. "They have a purpose now. That's what they need. A purpose."

"They need to work," he said.

"They are working," I replied. He shook his head. I kept going. "Look, farm labor is great. It demands a lot from them physically, and that's good. But if that's all they do, they will never be more than a labor pool. And they were already feeling that way."

"Guys always complain."

I pointed to the car. "While we've been standing here, they pushed that car over there, brought out the pressure washer, and cleaned it up. I didn't tell them to do that. You didn't tell them to do that. They did it on their own. Three months ago, they wouldn't have thought to do that or cared to do it even if they did think of it. And they wouldn't have been interested in doing it if we tried to make them."

"And you think working on that car changed their attitude?"

"I think working with a purpose—on a project that means something to them—did it. We can't just flog them into working. We have to give them a purpose for it."

He had a bitter expression. "But racing?"

"This isn't about making racers out of them. This is about teaching them how to find their way. Teaching them how to take a dream, break it down into its parts, and make it happen."

He sighed and shook his head again. "It's about getting someone killed."

"It's no riskier than working with farm machinery."

The laughter of the guys as they cleaned the car distracted us, and we never finished the conversation. After a moment, Lewis walked away, and I went over to the shop. The guys were finished with the car by then and gathered near a workbench.

"What do we do now?" Pete asked.

"Is the car clean?"

"Yes."

"Then push it over here."

"But we wrecked it," Palmer said. "Will it still work?"

And just like that, I made up my mind for good. No matter what, we were going racing. "The car has to be ready by the beginning of the season," I said. "So, push it over here, and let's get busy getting it ready."

Rick gave me a look. "What season?"

"Racing season."

"We're actually gonna race it?"

"That was the point, wasn't it?" I exclaimed.

"We thought it was just, you know, something to get our attention."

"We'll need to make a new fender for the front," Frank said. "I think the rest of it is okay."

"Push it over here," I repeated. "Let's have a look."

They brought the car to the shop and pushed it inside. I turned to Frank. "You and Gary get that fender off and get started on a new one."

Gary seemed bewildered. "Where would we get a new one?"

"Make it."

"Make it?"

"Yeah," I said. "Find a piece of sheet metal and form it into the shape of a fender."

"And then what?"

"Weld it into place."

Gary shook his head. "I don't know how to weld."

"I'll show you," I replied.

Pete was standing near the driver's window, arms across his chest, staring at the seat. I stood beside him. "Why do you think the car turned over?" I asked.

"I was driving too fast," he replied.

"Yes. But besides that. What else made it roll over?"

He glanced at the car and shrugged. "I don't know."

"It sits too high off the ground," I said.

"What difference does that make?"

"When you tried to turn to the left, the weight of the car shifted to the right."

He frowned. "The weight moved?"

"The force of it did," I explained. "The right side tried to turn, but the left side kept going straight."

His eyes opened wide in a look of realization. "And climbed over the right side?"

"Yeah." I grinned. "That's a good way to put it."

"Like Newton," he continued. "Object in motion stays in motion."

"Exactly. The right side changed direction—or tried to—but the left side kept coming."

"That's weird."

"What do you think we should do about that?" I asked.

"Well, if the car's too high, I guess we need to lower it. But how do we do that?"

"We need a different suspension system. And we need to stiffen up the right side."

"With what?"

I took him outside and pointed to the old truck we'd brought from the pasture. It was sitting by the concrete pad where we washed the car. "We'll use the springs from that," I said, pointing to it.

"They'll come off?"

"Sure they will," I replied. "Everything on that truck was put there, and everything can be removed. We just need the suspension system."

Through the remainder of the fall, we worked on getting the car in better shape. Using the hoist from the tractor, we picked up the truck and removed the front and rear suspension. It only had springs and shock absorbers—not traction bars or any of the more complex devices used today. With

George's help, we fabricated brackets and mounting points on the frame of the car, then bolted the truck springs in place. The shocks on the car weren't much better than those on the truck, but they didn't leak. So, we rigged them to work with the new springs.

Doing all of that lowered the car slightly but stiffened it quite a bit. We couldn't do much more and still comply with the rules. But tires remained an issue. Having wider tires would give us a better base for the weight to ride on and a wider footprint. It wouldn't seem like much to a casual observer, but a few inches of width at the four corners of the car would make a tremendous difference in how it handled. I just didn't know where we would find the money for it.

CHAPTER 14

The week after Thanksgiving, a letter arrived from Julia's mother. I opened it with apprehension and read it quickly. "Dear Jake, Father Deasy gave me your address. Julia has been sick for some time, and now she is dying. There is no one to care for David. He needs you. Please come." I stared at the page and read it again. The words sank deep into my soul.

Julia was the love of my life. Even then, after all that had happened, remembering the moment I saw her for the first time as a girl made something in me leap with anticipation. To think that she might die before we'd straightened things out between us…. The thought of it left me feeling hollow inside.

I read the letter once more. It was terse and stark, like every other conversation I'd had with Julia's mother since we told them Julia was pregnant. No hint of compassion. Not an ounce of kindness. Only the bare news. And a problem she wanted me to solve. David. I sighed at the thought of him.

We hadn't seen each other in over a year. Longer than that, actually. I barely knew him. He hardly knew me. Just a name. A face. Not much more. But he was my son, and his mother was dying, or so it seemed. I could never be sure about Julia's mother. She overstated everything regarding me. She might be overstating Julia's condition, too.

Father Deasy could confirm the details. If he gave them my address, he surely knew the situation. Under the circumstances, no one would object to me calling him from Lewis' office, so I started in that direction but as I walked through the barn, a fatherly instinct rose inside me. I hadn't felt like that in a long time, and suddenly, there it was. My son was in trouble. Someone had to rescue him, and that someone was me. Before I reached the office, I decided that regardless of the accuracy of the letter, I had to go there. To check on Julia and see about David. When I explained the situation to Lewis, and showed him the letter, he agreed I should find David and bring him back with me to the farm.

As best I could determine from the letter, David was living with Julia's parents, but there was no mention of where Julia might be. If she was nearing death, someone must be caring for her, and that would eliminate all of her family members except her mother. None of the rest of them would take her in. So, I packed a bag and headed towards New Orleans. If Julia was dying, there were things we needed to talk about. Things we needed to say. Things I needed to say. We couldn't let it end like we'd left it. I couldn't, anyway.

It was a tense trip for me, and all the way I battled flashbacks of incidents from the past. Julia calling to say she was pregnant. The two of us breaking the news to her parents. Then, telling mine. My father berating me for it. The tiny apartment and the excruciating financial struggle we experienced there. The day Julia walked out. Living on the street.

When I reached the city, I went straight to the house. Julia's mother met me at the door. I could tell from the way she looked at me that she didn't want me around. Not really. All she wanted was for me to solve the situation with David, whatever that was. She stepped aside and let me enter without any word of greeting.

In the living room, David was seated on the far end of the sofa, his eyes focused on a game he was playing through an electronic box that was connected to the television. I sat next to him and talked for a few minutes. I did most of the talking, raising questions about the game on the screen. The distance between us was palpable, but I did my best to engage him.

Between episodes of the game, I learned that after David and Julia moved to Slidell, he had remained there only a short time before returning to live with Julia's parents. Something about his mother's job, the roommate, a cramped lifestyle. I assumed the roommate didn't like having him around, but I didn't ask many questions about it.

Even with things as tense as they were in the living room, I was reluctant to go any farther. The stale, medicinal smell of illness was thick in the air. I was sure Julia was down the hall in her old bedroom, but I recoiled at the thought of seeing her there. Without asking, I knew that her condition was much worse than any letter could convey.

Finally, though, there was no way to avoid the issue at hand, so I excused myself from David and went to find Julia. She was lying in bed—the same one she'd used as a girl—with the covers up to her neck. Her eyes were sunken in their sockets. Her cheeks were hollow, the bones pressing against skin that was thin and colorless. She smiled when she saw me. "I knew you would come," she said. Her voice was weak.

"Your mother's letter sounded urgent."

"They say I don't have long."

Lymphoma. Discovered late. Spreading quickly. Her body deteriorating rapidly. As we talked, I had the sense she'd been hanging on the past few days to give me time to get there before the end. It was awful to see her like that. I choked back tears at first, but then we both cried. At the memory of what transpired between us and the thought of what might have been. Of moments had and moments lost.

The afternoon went by quickly as we talked, both of us desperate to reach across the gap the past had created, saying things we should have said long ago, knowing there would never be another chance to say them again. I apologized for the way we lived when we got married and for numbing myself with alcohol. She apologized for giving up and leaving.

By dinner time, Julia was exhausted. No one suggested

I stay and eat at the house, so I drove toward St. Dominic's and bought a hamburger at a café along the way. Father Deasy was at the rectory when I arrived. He offered me a room there, but I opted for the one at the parish hall, behind the kitchen where I'd slept before. I was glad to see him, but I needed space for myself right then. There was a lot for me to process.

The next morning, I awakened early and fixed toast and coffee in the parish kitchen, then drove to the house. When I went to Julia's bedroom, I found her condition had worsened. Her eyes were dull and listless. Her breathing was shallow and labored. The determination that had been present the day before was gone.

Despite her mother's disapproving looks, I sat with Julia all day. David came in to see her once or twice, and I took him to lunch at noon, but the remainder of the time I was seated in a chair beside her bed. I remained there through the evening, too, even though no one offered me dinner. And when the hour grew late, and the house fell silent, I stayed with her still, unwilling to leave her side.

About one in the morning, Julia's eyes opened wide, and she gasped as if startled or afraid. I thought she was gone, but she grabbed my hand and when I looked into her eyes, I could see she was alert but not afraid. "Tell David I love him," she whispered.

"I will."

"Tell him often."

"I will," I said once more. "But you can tell him yourself in a few hours."

She smiled. "I love you, Jake. I have always loved you."

"And I love you, Julia."

Her grip tightened on my hand, and she arched her back, pressing her shoulders against the mattress to take one more breath, then she relaxed and closed her eyes. A moment later, I felt her hand go limp in mine. I checked for a pulse but couldn't find one, so I went to the kitchen and phoned her doctor's answering service, then walked down the hall and tapped on the door to the bedroom where Julia's mother slept.

Two days after Julia died, Father Deasy conducted her funeral. That evening, I returned to the room in the parish hall. Not long after I arrived, Father Deasy joined me and we talked the way we had in the past, as if we'd never been apart. We talked about Julia and her mother. My parents. And eventually about my life on the street. That's when I learned a detective had been asking for me.

"What were they asking about?" I couldn't recall anything from my past that might have interested a detective.

"Apparently, there was a shooting several years ago," Deasy said.

"Where?"

"In the French Quarter," he said. "New information has come to light about it."

"What kind of information?"

"I don't know, but they think you know something that could help them."

A memory flashed through my mind—Pump, the car, the gunshots, the money in Pump's hand. "I didn't shoot anyone," I said.

"They didn't say you did."

"Then what do they want?"

"They have a video of you buying a bottle of whiskey," he said. "You paid for it with two twenties. The bills were counterfeit. They want to ask you about the money."

"Oh," I said, and I'm sure I sounded relieved, which I was. At least they didn't think I killed Pump. But the money was a problem.

If I told the police all that I knew about what happened that night, I would be admitting I stole from Pump. They might not pursue it against me, but I would also implicate myself in passing counterfeit currency when I paid for the whiskey, though I didn't know the money was fake. But that wasn't the worst of it. Telling the police all that I knew would suggest the guy in the car had something to do with the money, and that would cause serious trouble, especially if I told them who owned the car.

"They were here a few days ago," Deasy continued. "Parked on the street as if they were watching for someone."

"And you think they were waiting for me?"

"Yes," he replied. "They knew about Julia. I imagine they were watching the funeral, too, hoping to find you." When I didn't respond, he looked over at me. "Is there something you need to tell me, Jake?"

"That was a long time ago." My voice was soft and low.

"Would you like for me to hear your confession?"

"Yes," I said. "I would like that very much."

I sat on the edge of the bed. Father Deasy sat in a chair opposite me. "Bless me, Father," I began, "for I have sinned." Then I told him everything that happened that night in the French Quarter. Pump, the money, the whiskey. All of it. When I finished, Father Deasy laid his hand lightly atop my head and prayed the prayer of absolution.

When he finished, I looked over at him. "What do I do now?" I asked.

"That is your decision."

There was only one choice. I had to tell them what I knew, but I didn't have to go looking for them. They could come to me. "If they come around again," I said, "tell them I'll be glad to talk to them."

"Good."

We sat there for a while, neither of us saying anything, then I asked, "Does the past ever go away?"

He shook his head. "Not really, but it gets easier the farther you get from it."

"I suppose I'm not far enough away from it yet."

"Me either," he replied. "How are you doing with that sense of calling you used to discuss?"

"I haven't thought about it much until now," I replied. It was true. I hadn't. When I arrived at the farm it was all I could think of, but then I got busy and the issue of ordination receded. "I suppose with Julia no longer alive, the options might have changed, but I don't have the education the priesthood requires."

He nodded thoughtfully. "And you have a son."

I told him about the students, the shop, and how he hit upon the idea of a race car as a project. "It doesn't sound much like ministry, but it feels like it. The students have been really energized by what we're doing."

"Having a purpose makes all the difference," he noted.

"It has motivated them in every area," I said. "They study harder. Even on their own. Without being told to."

"Will they actually race this car?"

"That's the plan." I grinned. "This summer. If we can find some racing tires."

Father Deasy frowned. "Racing tires?"

"Race cars take special tires," I explained. "They're wider than the ones for the street. And the track we plan to race on is dirt. So, that's a special tire in itself."

"A special tire among special tires," he observed.

"Yes," I said. "They're special but not uncommon. Just expensive."

David and I remained in New Orleans for two more days,

then it was time to leave. On my way over to get him for the drive back to the farm, I stopped at the rectory to say good-bye to Father Deasy. A truck was parked in the driveway and Father Deasy stood beside it, talking to a man who appeared to be the driver. I parked near where they stood and got out.

As I approached them, Father Deasy said, "This is Bob. He owns a tire store in Laplace."

Bob and I shook hands. "So, you're thinking of getting into racing," he said.

"We're gonna try," I replied.

"Then this ought to help," he said as he climbed into the bed of the truck. I was puzzled at first, then I saw four racing tries lying in the truck. They were already mounted on rims. Bob handed one to me.

I took the tire and set it on the ground. "I don't have any way to pay you for this," I said.

"Not a problem," Father Deasy said with a smile. "Bob and I go way back. He made me a good deal on them."

I blinked back tears as Bob handed me a second tire. "We used to sponsor a car at the dragstrip in Houma. My brother had a car that ran on dirt at a track in Hammond." He handed me a third tire and grinned. "You're gonna have a lot of fun."

CHAPTER 15

The drive back from New Orleans to the farm was uneventful. David sat on his side of the truck. I sat at the steering wheel. I tried to talk to him but after three or four attempts fell flat, I gave up and we rode in silence. A few hours later, we arrived at the cottage. It was late in the day. I showed David to his room. We brought our things in from the truck and mostly kept to ourselves.

For dinner that evening, we went to a café on the highway. They had a pretty good hamburger, and we ate well. David seemed to enjoy it. I tried again to talk to him, but he didn't have much to say, and I didn't push him. It had been a long day. We both were tired.

The next morning, we ate breakfast early and left for my usual trip to St. Francis Church in Alexandria for early morning Mass. Frank went with us. He tried to make friends with David during the ride, but David showed little interest. He'd already let me know he didn't want to attend Mass, or school, or be with me on the farm. I knew what he meant—that he missed his mother and the life he'd known with her parents—but neither of us could do anything about that.

After Mass, I took David to school and enrolled him. We met several people including the school counselor, Susan Gilbert. She helped David determine which bus to ride home in the afternoon and where to get off on the route, then she gave him a class schedule and we followed her to his homeroom. Along the way, she offered to monitor David's progress through the remainder of the year. "Mid-term transfers are difficult," she noted. "They sometimes need extra help adjusting." I was grateful for her kindness that morning but didn't expect to ever see her again.

When David was set at school, Frank and I started back toward the farm. He looked over at me. "Do you think David knows how to find that bus stop?"

I shrugged. "I guess so. The driver will help him."

"What's he gonna do then?"

"When?"

"After he gets home."

"Hang out at the house until I get there, I suppose."

Frank seemed troubled. "He's gonna hang out there, at the house where you stay, by himself?"

"It'll only be for two hours."

"Yeah." Frank grinned. "Two hours alone, listening to music and playing video games." He looked over at me again. "You do have video games, don't you?"

"I don't know." I shrugged. "I never checked."

Frank shook his head. "You better pick up your game, Dad."

Frank's comments left me wondering if I was doing the right thing with David, expecting him to fend for himself in the late afternoon, but I didn't feel comfortable having him at the shop with the guys and the staff. Not yet. Maybe later. But not right then.

When Frank and I arrived back at the farm, I saw a car parked near the barn. A nondescript dark green sedan with government plates. I had a sinking feeling in the pit of my stomach. Frank's eyes were wide and alert. "That's a detective's car," he said.

"Looks like it," I responded.

"Why do they do that?"

"Do what?"

"Drive cars that look like that." He pointed to it. "They call them unmarked, but they're always that color and they always have that little antenna by the rear glass." He pointed again. "See it?"

"Yeah."

"And black wall tires, too. And they even have that Police Interceptor logo on the trunk lid. Like it's not obvious enough, they gotta put the name right there for everyone to see. And a spotlight hanging off the driver's side mirror." He was animated. "Might as well get on the loudspeaker and announce, 'Look at me. I'm a cop.'"

He had a point. Today, they drive less noticeable vehicles, but in the 80s, they were obvious for their plainness. A marked version of an unmarked car.

I parked the pickup truck at the shop and a few minutes later, the guys arrived for the morning session. We put our project car on jacks and began changing the street tires for the racing tires I brought back from New Orleans. The front ones had plenty of room to fit beneath the fenders, but the rear ones were too wide to go beneath the car body. We were discussing how to fix it when Lewis appeared. A man in a business suit accompanied him. The guys retreated as they approached me, having recognized the stranger as a cop.

"This is Lovell Aldrich," Lewis said to me. "He's a detective with the New Orleans police department. He wants to ask you some questions."

Aldrich gestured toward the door. "Why don't we step outside. Might be easier to talk out there."

I followed him from the shop, and we stood near his car. Before he could speak, I said, "Father Deasy sent you?"

"He told me where to find you."

"How can I help?"

Aldrich removed a photograph from his pocket and showed it to me. "This was taken from surveillance video at a liquor store in the French Quarter." He pointed to a person in the picture. "Several people say that's you."

I glanced at the image. "Not much doubt about that," I said. And there wasn't. I was skinnier then, with hollow eyes and greasy hair, but anyone who knew me from the street would know it was me.

"According to store records, you bought a quart of Jack Daniels. Paid for it with two twenty-dollar bills. Do you remember anything like that?"

"I bought a lot of Jack Daniels back in the day, but that was a long time ago." I didn't want to say too much until I knew what he was really interested in. "Father Deasy said those twenties might have been counterfeit." I handed him the photo. "Is that what you wanted to know about?"

"What can you tell me about them?"

"Not much."

"Do you know where they came from, or where you got them?"

"I don't know if the twenties I remember are the same ones you're asking about, but here's what I know. One night, when I was living on the street in the Quarter, I was stumbling along looking for something to sell, something to eat, something to drink. Just looking. And a blue BMW went by. It came to a stop a little way down the street. A drug dealer named Pump approached the driver's side of the car. I hadn't even noticed him before. He must have been standing in the shadows, waiting for whoever was in the car."

"The drug dealer?"

"Yeah. Looked like he had been waiting on the opposite

side of the street from me, but I didn't notice him until he walked up to the car."

"And his name was Pump?"

"That's what everybody called him. I think his real name was Ricardo. I never knew his last name."

"Then what happened?"

"The way the car rolled up, and with Pump hiding in the shadows, I figured it was a drug deal. So, I hung back, trying to stay out of the way and not be seen. I was hoping Pump might give me a few dollars after it was over, so I could get something to drink. Then I heard a gunshot. I think it was two shots. Might have been three. The muzzle flash lit up the place and I could see Pump's face." I tried not to tell him about the car, but I knew he was going to ask.

And sure enough, just as I expected, he said, "What about the person in the car?"

"His head never came out and from the angle where I was standing, I couldn't see who it was."

That was true, I couldn't see him, but I'd seen that car hundreds of times and I knew who it belonged to, I just didn't want to say. Eddie could be nasty when he got upset and telling the cops about what he'd been doing would have upset him.

"Okay," Aldrich said. "There were gunshots. And then what?"

"Pump staggered back from the car, grabbing at his chest. Fell to the ground. The car drove away. When it was gone, I walked over to where Pump was lying. As best I could tell, he was already dead. Couple of holes in his chest. Blood oozing out. I didn't think he could be alive."

"And then what happened?"

I felt bad about what I did next, but I had already told him most of it, so I told him the rest. "I saw a roll of twenty-dollar bills in Pump's hand. His fist was still clenched around it. So, I peeled back his fingers, took the money, and walked away."

"Was it difficult to get his fingers out of the way?"

"No," I said. "They were just there because that's the last place they'd been."

"What street were you on?"

"Toulouse, I think."

"When the car drove away, which way did it go?"

"Towards the river. But look," I added quickly, "I didn't know the bills were counterfeit. I was just a drunk trying to get a drink."

"Other than the liquor store, where else did you spend the money?"

"Nowhere that I remember. I bought the whiskey, drank it, and fell asleep. Woke up on a bench across from the cathedral."

"At Jackson Square?"

"Yes. Across from St. Louis Cathedral. When I woke up, Father Deasy was sitting beside me. He took me to St. Dominic's, gave me a place to stay, straightened me out."

"And that's it?"

"Yes," I replied. "That's it."

"And you bought the whiskey the same night the drug dealer was shot?"

"Yes."

"Was anyone with you?"

"It seems like someone might have been with me when I left the liquor store, but I don't remember who it was. There were always people hanging around, looking for something to drink. And when somebody bought something, they'd all gather around for a sip."

"Do you remember anyone specifically being there?"

"No," I said. "But when I woke up and Father Deasy was there with me on the bench, the bottle was empty. It had only been a couple of hours since I bought it. That's a lot to drink in that amount of time, even for me, back then."

"But you don't remember anyone specifically, other than Father Deasy?" Aldrich asked. "Or who it might have been?"

"No," I replied. "Sorry."

"Who else knows you're here?"

"Here? At the farm?"

"Yes," he said. "Who else knows you're up here?"

"Father Deasy. My in-laws. The priest in Alexandria. My son is up here with me now. The school he attends has my address. I talked to a few people there. They know where we live. And I suppose my mother and sisters might know."

"Are you in regular contact with them?"

"No," I said. "But they have a way of finding out where I am. Why?"

"The Treasury Department thinks those twenty-dollar bills came from a counterfeit ring that they've been after for years."

I didn't like the sound of that. "Am I in danger?"

"I couldn't say for sure," Aldrich replied. "But we'll let you know if something specific comes up." He turned to leave. "I'll be in touch. We'll probably need to talk again, I imagine."

When Aldrich was gone, I returned to the shop. The guys were standing near the door, waiting for me. Apparently, they'd been listening to the conversation. They howled and laughed as I came in.

"The past is catching up to you," Pete laughed.

"It has a way of doing that," Ron added.

"And now," Rick said, "you got the man on your back."

They all laughed and slapped me on the shoulder like we were comrades, but I was concerned. Counterfeit. Organized crime. Questions from a city detective. Dredging up events from several years earlier. The whole thing left me worried, especially with David around.

The next afternoon, George didn't have much for the guys to do, so I had them load four worn-out tractor tires into the back of a farm truck and we rode through the pasture, marking off the four turning points of a half-mile oval with the tires. When they were in place, we returned to the shop.

I found a straw broom and pulled twelve strands from it, then cut the strands into different lengths. Holding them level with my fist, I said, "Okay, guys, let's draw straws."

"What for?"

"To see who goes first," I replied.

"Goes first for what?"

"To drive the car around that course we just laid out."

Pete drew the shortest straw, which meant he drove the car from the shop to the field. As he approached the course, I motioned for him to stop, then reached through the window and turned off the engine. "Okay, now you get to do some of the fun stuff. Three laps for each of you around the course. Start slow. Keep the car under control. This is practice. Just get the car around the course three times without wrecking it." Everyone laughed at the memory of Pete's earlier experience rolling the car on its side.

When Pete was strapped into the safety harness, with the helmet in place on his head, he started the car again. I stepped out of the way, and Pete drove onto the course. He made it three times around the tires without wrecking, then the next person took a turn.

They spent the afternoon going round and round the tires. Everyone had multiple turns. I did my best to coach them, but they were having so much fun it was difficult to get their attention.

As the sun was beginning to set, I glanced away and saw David standing at the edge of the woods. He was watching us, and I wanted to include him, but I wasn't sure I should.

CHAPTER 16

As the end of the year approached, life had settled into a routine. I drove David to school in the morning when Frank and I went to Mass. He rode the bus home in the afternoon, and we had dinner together in the early evening. On Saturdays and Sundays, we hung out at the house or went to Alexandria. He didn't seem particularly excited about our arrangement, but he wasn't angry about it, either.

On Christmas Day, we began our celebration at the cottage. I bought a new television and game console, with several games. We played games together most of the morning. At noon, we went to the farmhouse and ate lunch with the guys. Jessica joined us. David seemed to enjoy talking to her, and that helped him ease into relating with the guys. It was a pleasant afternoon.

The following day, I took David to New Orleans to see his grandparents. We spent two nights there—David with Julia's parents, me in the room off the kitchen in the parish hall. I didn't like being away from him, and I didn't like that he was under their influence again, but they made it clear

I wasn't invited to stay at their house. On the positive side, staying at the parish hall gave me time with Father Deasy, which was always helpful.

The morning we were leaving to return to the farm, I went to the house and picked up David, then came back to the rectory to say goodbye to Father Deasy. As we were leaving, Lovell Aldrich arrived. "We need to talk," he said.

Father Deasy took David inside. Aldrich and I stood near the truck and he showed me a grainy photograph of a car that appeared to be a BMW. "We got this from a security camera on the corner of Toulouse and Royal. Any chance it's the car you saw?"

"It might be," I replied. "But I don't know if it's the exact one. Did this come from the night Pump got shot?" It seemed impossible that anyone would have a videotape from that long ago.

Aldrich ignored my question. "Is there anything you can tell me about the driver?" he asked.

"Like I said before, I didn't see much of him. Just a glimpse of the side of his face, maybe. And his hand when it came out the window with the gun." Lying to a cop was a serious offense, but I didn't want Eddie to find out I said anything.

"But you could see him," Aldrich said.

"Only for an instant. In the muzzle flash."

"What did you see?" he asked. "Think. I need you to think. What did you see?"

I closed my eyes and replayed the scene in my mind. Pump. The hand. The gun. The shot. My eyes popped open. "The driver was wearing one of those big wristwatches," I said. "Like a Rolex or something like that."

Aldrich grinned as he handed me another photograph, apparently taken from the same video as the first, showing a view of the driver through the front windshield. His left hand gripped the steering wheel and on his wrist was a large watch. Aldrich pointed to it. "Was he wearing a watch like that one?"

"Yeah," I said. "Like that one." I handed the photo to him. "But I have no idea if the guy in the car that night was the same guy in that picture."

"That's okay." He was smiling as he returned the photos to his pocket.

I was curious. "This happened several years ago." I couldn't remember exactly how long it had been. "Why are you interested in it now?"

"The car in the picture is registered to Eddie Morrisette."

"The mayor's son?" I did my best to sound surprised.

"Yeah."

"Was that him driving it?"

Aldrich nodded. "We think so."

"But there's no way anyone still has video from the night Pump was killed." They didn't have many cameras in the French Quarter back then. Club owners thought it would dampen their business if people knew they were being recorded.

"It's Morrisette," Aldrich said. "And it's his car. We know it for a fact."

That seemed like a stretch if they were trying to make a criminal case against Eddie, but I didn't argue. "You must be investigating something bigger than a drug deal from two or three years ago."

"We think Eddie's involved in a big operation."

"How big?"

"Big."

He wasn't giving up much, and neither was I. "You think Eddie's involvement might have some influence on the mayor?"

Aldrich raised an eyebrow. "We think the mayor might be involved."

I was pretty sure that wasn't right. "Did you talk to Eddie?"

Aldrich shook his head. "We're not ready for that yet. And besides, we can't find him. Any idea where he might be?"

"No," I replied. "I didn't know him." It was true. I used to see Eddie often, but we weren't friends.

Aldrich shook my hand. "If you hear anything, let me know. And keep your eyes open up there. You're the first person we've found with anything that ties Eddie to any of this."

"I'm not sure I can tie anyone to anything," I responded.

"You've gotten us closer than we've been so far."

I didn't like the sound of that. Eddie wasn't the sort of guy you wanted to inform on. He had a reputation for being brutal with people who talked about his business, and word always had a way of getting back. Simply talking to Aldrich in the rectory driveway might be enough to cause trouble, so I got David from the rectory, and we hit the road.

A week or two after Christmas break ended, I received a letter from the school counselor telling me David wasn't doing well in class. If he continued to perform as he had, he wouldn't pass for the year. That evening after work, I tried to talk to David about it, but he was non-responsive. I pleaded, cajoled, and demanded, but he refused to engage the topic.

Finally, I dropped onto a chair at the table and propped my head against my hand. "I don't understand," I said. "Can't we at least talk about this?"

"Why?" he said at last.

"Because school is important."

"Why do you care?" He had a snotty tone. "You'll just leave again."

That comment stabbed me in the heart. I took a deep breath, hoping to avoid a nasty retort. "What makes you say that?"

"That's what Grandma says."

Grandma. Julia's mother. The mention of her brought a flood of emotion. I pushed it aside as best I could. "She told you I would leave you?"

"I overheard her talking to Grandpa. She said you left Mom." He looked over at me. "And you left me."

That was the most painful comment of all. I hadn't left Julia, she left me. And she took David with her when she went. But I had tried to reach her after that. Even met with her on a few occasions. I had not done much of that with David, even though, as his father, I could have demanded to see him, and no one could have stopped me.

"It was a difficult time for everyone," I said. I didn't want to tell him Julia was the one who broke us up. Not now. Not with all the disruption her death had brought.

"Isn't that what happened?"

"Not exactly."

"But you were gone."

"Yes. I was gone."

"And now Mama's gone."

"Yes."

"And Grandpa will be dead soon." He started crying. "And so will Grandma."

I took him in my arms. He pushed against me to get away, but I hugged him and finally, he rested his head on my shoulder. "Everyone leaves," he sobbed.

"Whatever trouble your mother and I had was a long time ago," I said. "I'm not leaving."

"How do I know that?"

"You don't."

He leaned away and looked at me. "Then what do I do?"

"We'll have to face up to what's in front of us and deal with it. And right now, that means dealing with each other."

"Okay."

"And dealing with school."

Reluctantly, he put aside the video games and music and began to focus on schoolwork, but I knew he was only doing it because I had confronted him. And because the counselor had written to say he was failing. Like the guys in the group, he needed a positive reason for it. Something that could motivate him to want to learn. And as I thought about that over the next few days, I realized I already had something that would do that very thing—the race car. If it worked for the guys in the group, it would work for David.

Later that week, I took the guys back to the course we'd laid out with the tires in the pasture behind the barn. This time, I had a stopwatch and a clipboard. They took turns, seeing how fast they could drive the course. I timed their attempts with the stopwatch and noted the results on the clipboard.

When about half the guys had taken a turn, it was time for David to be home from school. I sent Frank to the cottage to get him. They came to the pasture. I handed David the clipboard and told him to record the times as I read them from the stopwatch.

After everyone had taken a turn with the car, I looked over at David. "Do you want a turn?"

"Doing what?"

"Driving the car," I said.

His eyes were open wide in a look of surprise. "I don't know how to drive."

"You'll learn." I took the clipboard from him. "Get in the car."

"Yeah," Pete said. "Give the kid a turn."

Frank ushered him toward the car. "You'll do good," he said. "Nothing to worry about."

David smiled back at me. "Are you sure it's okay?"

"Yes," I said. "It's fine."

Frank helped David into the car and showed him how to buckle the safety harness, then handed him the helmet. I leaned down to see through the window. "The tires mark the turns. You can see where they guys have been running. Take three easy laps. Nothing fancy. Just get the car around the course." He nodded and I gave him a pat on the shoulder.

Frank reached through the window and turned the key to start the car, then showed him how to put the transmission in gear. We all watched as David slowly made his way around the course. He laughed the entire time. The guys cheered and shouted.

Near the end of the week, Susan Gilbert, the counselor from David's school, came to the farm. We talked outside the shop and after a discussion of David's poor performance she said, "I wonder if drugs may be part of David's problem."

The way she glanced around as she spoke told me our program was the basis of her suspicion. It aggravated me, but I squelched the urge to defend the guys. "I don't think so," I replied.

"Would you recognize it if it was?" she asked.

"I'm sure I would."

"You don't think some of the guys in your program might be supplying him?"

And there it was. The obvious. The easy. The lazy approach. "If he's using drugs," I said, "he's not getting it from around here. These men are ex-addicts, not current users. They have very little opportunity to get anything. And even if they did, David isn't with them except in the afternoons."

She looked skeptical. "That you know of."

"Why do you think he's using?"

"Poor academic performance is one of the signs."

When I first met Susan, I had been attracted to her, but hearing her glib assessment of David and his situation offended me and I began to consider her differently. There was so much more going on in his life, things she knew nothing about, and right then, I didn't want to tell her about it.

No one needed to know the trouble he'd experienced. The trauma. The challenges.

I looked past the barn to the pasture, trying to think of a polite way to tell her to leave, when I realized it might be helpful for her to know about David's life—and telling her would put her in her place. So, instead of escorting her off the property, I gave her a brief sketch of all we'd been through. My story. David's story. Julia's death. And how we came to be at the farm.

By the time I was through, her expression had changed from confident to sorrowful. "That's a lot for someone to endure."

"Especially as young as he is."

She looked at me. "For anyone of any age." There was a kindness in her voice I hadn't heard in a long time.

"Yeah." I glanced away, avoiding her gaze. Feeling suddenly small and useless. "Whatever happened to me, I brought most of it on myself. David didn't. He was just a kid." She touched my elbow. I smiled at her. It was a moment, but I let it go. "Can he make up the work?" I asked.

"He is so far behind," she said, "I doubt he can catch up by the end of the year."

"What about summer school?"

"That might work if he was behind in a single subject, but he's behind in all of his subjects."

"What should we do?"

"I think he'll need to repeat the grade."

That didn't seem like a good option. "Is there some way you or someone else can help him?"

"A tutor might help. Would you like me to suggest someone?"

I thought of Jessica. "No," I replied. "I think I know who to get."

When Susan left, I walked up to the house and talked to Jessica about tutoring David. She agreed to work with him after he came home from school. I suggested they meet at the cottage. She agreed.

That night, while we ate dinner, I told David about my conversation with Susan and the arrangement with Jessica. He wasn't too happy about it. "If I'm with her, I can't drive the car with the guys."

Driving the car was something he enjoyed, but I hadn't thought of that when I talked to Jessica. "What if we drove the car on Saturdays," I suggested.

"What if we didn't have a tutor every day?" David countered.

I liked that he responded, and it made me grin. "What if you meet with Jessica and get started on your classes. We can drive the car on Saturdays, and we'll see how it goes with Jessica?"

He laughed. "Okay."

CHAPTER 17

Through the remainder of the winter, the students continued to drive the car on the course in the pasture, and each day their times improved, but as spring drew near, farm work increased. Time spent preparing the car was confined to class sessions in the morning and afternoon. Driving the car was moved to Saturday afternoon for everyone, which suited David perfectly. He enjoyed being with the guys as much as being in the car.

In the shop, our discussions moved on from mechanical parts of the car to work on the car's exterior. Forming sheet metal to replace damaged fenders, beating out dents, that sort of thing. In order to race the car on a track, we had to remove the glass from it, including the lights, which meant the light cavities had to be covered. That's where our lessons began. George helped them with some of it, but as farm work increased, he had less and less time to spare. Race day wasn't far off, and there still was a lot to do. Bodywork, mostly, but also a trailer to haul the car to the track. I was worried we would never get it all done in time.

Work on the car's sheet metal proved less challenging than I anticipated, and when it was finished, we turned to the task of painting the car. That meant sanding it, removing the rust, papering and taping the holes where the windows had been, which brought up the question of color. All of the guys had ideas about what colors the car should be, but I insisted it had to be red and gold. "I've already registered the car at the track," I explained. "That's the color I gave them. Red with gold trim."

Pete seemed surprised. "You registered the car?"

"How else are we gonna race?"

Rick spoke up. "What else did they want to know?"

"They asked about a driver, but I put them off. We can tell them that when we get to the track. And they gave me our number."

Pete frowned. "A number?"

"Every car has a number," Frank said. "It goes on the side."

Gary called out from the opposite side of the car. "We're actually taking this car to a track?"

"Yes," I replied. "I've told you that two or three times."

"When?"

"The first Saturday in June."

Pete's mouth fell open in a look of disbelief. Everyone else stopped what they were doing and came around to where I was standing. "That's not far off," Pete said, finally. "Who's gonna drive?"

"We'll rank everyone by their time on the course in the pasture," I said. "Whichever one of you is the fastest in the pasture gets to drive first on the track. We'll change drivers every week. Work our way through the group."

"Everyone gets a turn?"

"Yes," I said. "Everyone gets a turn."

Gary was beside me then. "What's the car number?"

"Eight," I said.

"I like nine," Rick offered.

"What about fifteen," Ron suggested.

"It's not a choice," I said, cutting them off. "The number was assigned by the people at the track."

Frank grinned. "You really told them we were coming?"

"I told them we intend to."

The final task in preparing the car was to add the lettering—painting the car's number on the sides and roof and writing the names of our sponsors. We only had one, an unofficial sponsorship from Father Deasy's friend, Bob—the man who supplied our first set of tires. I found some pictures from a racing magazine that showed what other race cars looked like and checked the rulebook to make sure we did it correctly.

We began with the sponsor's name, and for two weeks each of the guys took a turn trying to hand-paint the words

'Bob's Construction' on the rear section of the car, in the space between the tire and the end of the car. Though they gave it their best, none of them had a hand steady enough to get it right.

Then David showed up one afternoon after his tutoring session with Jessica. Frank suggested I give him a turn at the lettering. To my surprise, his hand was steady. His letters were perfect.

When David finished with the name, he added the car number on either side and on the top. As a final touch, I had him put the names of the guys, including his own, on the rear roof supports.

As it turned out, David didn't need Jessica's help as much as we thought. Three days each week was more than enough. They also moved their tutoring location from the cottage to the house where the guys lived. I liked that better, too.

Every Monday, Wednesday, and Friday, David got off the school bus at the road and walked to the house to study. His grades improved immediately and rose steadily through the semester. Midway through the term, Susan, the school counselor, sent a note asking me to schedule an appointment. A few days later, I phoned her. "Is there a problem with David?"

"No," she replied. "He's doing quite well. I just wanted to know what you did to help him."

"We have a lady who comes to the farm to teach the guys in our program. I arranged for her to tutor him in the afternoons. And I limited his time at night with music and video games."

"How did you get him to agree with that?"

"The guys in the program have been building a car in the shop. They drive it on a course we marked in the pasture. I let David take a turn one day and he really liked it. So, I told him if he wanted to keep driving the car, his grades had to improve."

"Interesting," she replied. "And this person who tutors him, is she a certified teacher?"

"She's a college student. Studying to be a teacher, I think. She does a good job with the guys. You should come out to the farm and meet her."

That Friday afternoon, Susan came to the farm. I introduced her to Jessica, and we reviewed David's work. Susan was impressed. "He might pass if he keeps this up."

When we came from the house, she noticed the car through the open doors of the shop. "That's the car you were telling me about?"

"That's it," I said.

"It looks like a race car."

"It is."

"Where did you get it?"

"The guys made it."

"Your students made that?"

"They began with a regular car," I said. "But it was in bad shape."

"And it runs."

"Sure." I grinned. "Wouldn't be a race car if it didn't."

By then we were at the shop, and she walked around the car, checking it out. "They did a great job." She glanced back at me. "You've done this before?"

"No. But they needed a project, and this seemed like a good fit."

"And you really intend to race it?"

"That's the plan."

"Where?"

"Tioga Speedway."

"My dad and uncles used to go there sometimes." She looked over at me again. "Who's going to drive it?"

"One of the students."

She raised an eyebrow. "Do they know how to drive a car in a race?"

"We've been practicing in the field behind the barn."

She had a wary expression. "You know that's not the same, right?"

"I know they can't learn by reading about it."

She leaned inside the car. "And your students put this together?" she asked, pointing to the dash. It was obviously not standard.

"They had help with some of it. The farm manager is good with sheet metal."

"You have a dozen guys in the program. How will you choose which one gets to drive?"

"We'll start with the ones who've been the fastest on the practice course."

Practice course. That made me grin. It was four old tractor tires in a pasture, but talking to her made me nervous.

She ran her fingers lightly over the lettering on the roof post. "David painted those names," I volunteered. "And the sponsor's name. And the number on the side."

She seemed impressed. "He did that?"

"Without a stencil," I said proudly. "And without drawing it first. Just freehanded it."

"Impressive."

"I thought so."

"He might be interested in art."

"Maybe," I said. "I'll ask him about it."

I thought he might be interested in art, too, but I wanted to avoid the parental trap of pushing a kid toward everything that seemed to interest him. Some things in life are meant to indicate career potential, and some things are meant to be pleasurable and nothing more. The distinction was one for David to discover for himself.

When we'd seen all there was to see in the shop, I walked with her to her car. "Listen," I said. "Don't say anything to David about how well he's doing with his classwork."

She frowned. "Why not?"

"I want him to finish well this year. And I want him to

continue working with Jessica through the summer."

"That's a good idea."

We were at her car, and I held the door for her while she got inside. "Maybe you'll come watch us race," I suggested.

"When is it?"

"The first Saturday night in June."

She laughed. "That might be interesting."

"I'm sure it will be," I said. "But if you come, wear something you don't mind getting dirty. It's a dirt track."

CHAPTER 18

Spring brought increasingly warmer weather and an increasingly laborious schedule of farm work. By then, Lewis had hired a new group leader—Tommy, from Shreveport. With him to help, I didn't have to go to the field with the guys, but the demands on their time and energy took a toll on other aspects of the program. Keeping them focused on the lessons necessary for obtaining a GED, sorting out their options for the future…and learning to drive the car was a challenge. At last, however, we made it to summer and David finished the academic year in public school with passing grades.

One of the guys and George worked at night to build a trailer for the car using the frame and axles of a mobile home and on the first Saturday in June, we connected it to the hitch on my pickup. When it was safely in place, we rolled the race car from the shop and loaded it on the trailer. I pulled it around to the farm's gas pump and filled the car's tank, then gathered everyone by the shop.

"When we get to the track, things might be a little hectic.

So, before we go, I want you to know I'm proud of the way you've worked—on the car, on learning to drive it, and the way you did that and got all the rest done, too."

"Speaking of which," Gary said. "Who's going to drive the car in the race? You never said."

"Pete," I replied. "He was the fastest." They slapped him on the back and seemed genuinely glad for him. "This will be a new experience for all of us," I continued. "And while we're enjoying it, let's remember to keep our mind on our business. We're going to the track to have fun and compete with the other cars and drivers, but it's just as important to those other drivers as it is to us. So, remember to be courteous. And whether we win tonight or win the championship, we're there to learn."

Pete's eyes opened wide. "Championship? What championship?"

"Every car in the race is awarded points based on the finishing order," I explained. "The higher you finish, the more points you get. At the end of the season, the car with the most points in each division wins the championship. Big trophy. Lots of celebration."

Rick grinned. "Do you think we could win it?"

"If they give points for best car," Frank offered, "we've already won."

"Exactly," I said. "Winning a race is the lesser of our goals."

While we were talking, George arrived in an SUV. He

parked beside us and when I finished talking with the guys, I pointed in his direction. "Some of you can ride with George. Some of you can go in the truck with me. Everybody, find a seat."

When we arrived at the track, a steward—one of the track officials who helped conduct the race—showed us where to park in the infield. While we unloaded the car, the Modifieds began their qualifying laps. They were loud and fast with experienced drivers who knew how to glide the car around the track in a smooth circle as big as the track dimensions allowed, a method that kept the car's engine running at full throttle all the way around.

Pete watched as they went by. I came alongside him. "They're good," I noted.

"Think I can do that with ours?"

"That's the goal," I said. "But you'll have to work your way up to it. These guys have been racing for a long time. Steering the car is something they don't have to think about."

"I just hope I don't roll it over."

"Well," I said. "If you do, we already know how to put it back together."

While the Modifieds were still on the track, a second steward arrived with a clipboard. "Who's your driver?" he asked, looking to me for an answer.

"Pete," I said, pointing.

The steward noted Pete's name on his chart. "We use an inverted start," he said, talking to Pete. "You'll make a qualifying run, then we'll line you up with the fastest cars in the back. Slowest cars in front. No sandbagging."

Pete frowned. "What does that mean?" I had forgotten to explain this part to them.

"It means," the steward said, "if your lap time during the race is more than a quarter of a second faster than your qualifying time, you'll be disqualified."

"Okay."

The steward continued. "When the Modifieds finish qualifying, we'll do the Late Models. When they're finished, line your car up over there." He pointed. "Bombers get two laps to qualify. Got it?"

"Yes, sir," Pete replied.

It took almost an hour for the Modifieds and Late Models to finish qualifying. When it was time for the Bombers, Pete climbed into the car and buckled himself into the driver's seat. Frank made sure the helmet was strapped tightly in place, then Pete flipped the switch and started the engine. I was glad to hear it running without any trouble.

As Pete drove at an idle through the infield, I walked along with him. It was a surreal moment for me. Racing. With a car that I helped build. On a track with a group of former drug addicts. I could not have imagined it when I first left St Dominic's.

Pete steered the car into line with the others in our class and brought it to a stop. I leaned down to the window. "Remember," I said. "Keep it smooth, but try to make it fast."

"Right," he said with a nod.

"Drive it like we've been practicing. Straight on the straightaways. Kick the rear out in the curves."

Pete nodded again. I gave his arm an encouraging squeeze and backed away. David appeared beside me. "Jessica is here," he said, pointing.

Bleachers lined the front stretch and I saw her sitting with Mike, the group leader. While I was watching them, Susan Gilbert appeared, dressed in jeans and a t-shirt. She made her way in their direction and sat down next to Jessica. Even from a distance, she looked great. I was mesmerized by her appearance and stared at her until David nudged me again and pointed to the track. Pete was beginning his qualifying laps.

Although the car looked good, the first lap was unusually slow. The second was quicker but still slower than any other car in the class. I knew he would be embarrassed and began thinking of things to say to encourage him.

When Pete completed his final lap, he drove the car to the infield and started toward me but one of the stewards motioned for him to park near the track entrance. David and I walked over to where he was parked.

"Why did they tell me to stop here?" Pete asked.

"Our class goes first."

"First?"

"The crowd came to see the Modifieds," I explained. "They'll go last so everyone will stay to the end."

He looked confused. "What do I do now?"

"Sit in the car and wait," I said.

Pete still seemed puzzled. "Why did they put me here?" he asked. "Shouldn't the car that's going first be up here?"

I grinned. "You're that car."

He frowned. "Me?"

"You're the slowest in the field," I said. "So, with an inverted start, you get the inside position on the front row."

"Oh. I didn't realize that's what it meant."

"You'll be on the inside of the front row."

He looked worried. "But that means I have to lead the others."

"Right."

"But I don't know what to do."

There had been so much to tell them and so much to do just to get the car prepared I had forgotten to tell them the mechanics of how a race was conducted. Most of them had never even watched a race on television.

"The pace car will lead you around the track for a lap or two," I said. "To get all the cars lined up on the track. Then the pace car will pull out of the way, and you'll set the pace to the green flag."

"How do I do that?"

"Stay even with the car next to you and watch the guy in the flag stand." I pointed to it. "When he waves the green flag, press the gas pedal and start racing."

"So, I'll already be moving when we start."

"Yes," I replied. "Don't worry about how fast you're going, or how it looks, or whether someone else thinks you're doing it right. This isn't the Indianapolis 500. Just drive like you're in the pasture and try not to hit anyone."

With the cars together and ready to go, it became obvious to me that our car looked better than any of them. Ours was painted and trimmed and had matching rims for the wheels. Our sponsor was noted on the rear fenders. The number was painted in the correct place and in the correct proportions. The other cars were a mottled group. Some were painted primer gray, others with fenders of one color and a hood of another with their numbers only more or less correct. Many had no mention of sponsors or crew members at all and seemed to have dents and scrapes from the year before. I was certain that, merely from appearances, we had raised the expectations of our fellow drivers far beyond our ability to perform.

When the cars were in the proper order, a steward motioned to Pete, and he drove onto the track. The car beside him did as well and the rest followed. It was a large field—twenty-eight cars in total—aligned two-by-two forming a double file.

Before they reached the first turn, the pace car came

from the infield and moved in front of them. As they slowly made their way around the track, David and I hurried back to where the guys were waiting and watching. We all climbed into the bed of the truck and stood for a better view.

The cars completed the first lap with the pace car, but as they came around a second time and turned toward the front stretch, the pace car scooted out of the way and coasted into the infield. The flagman waited a moment, allowing the cars to come partway toward him, then waved the green flag. Pete slowly increased his speed, but not by very much. Cars behind him crowded against each other, the faster ones trying to avoid running over the slower ones in front.

The cars remained side by side through the first turn and continued like that for several laps. Pete wasn't very fast, but he held his position on the inside lane, and no one could get around him. About five laps into the race, Pete seemed to get comfortable with the car and increased his speed. Momentum from the extra speed caused the car to slide up the track at the center of the turn. One of the cars from the back made a run up the outside of the pack and as our car pushed up, it collided with that car, sending it off the course and into the bushes beyond the track.

With the car off the course, a yellow light came on and the flagman waved a yellow flag, a signal to the field to slow down and maintain their positions while officials tended to the wreck. Pete knew nothing about that, and I watched in horror as he ignored the light and flag. He kept going at the same speed he'd been before, caught up with the rear of the field, and slammed into a car that was the fastest in the class.

The flagman pointed to Pete and waved a black flag, indicating our car had been disqualified from the race. Pete didn't know what that flag meant, either, and continued around the track for two more laps.

One of the infield stewards came to the truck where we were standing. "Get that car off the track!" he shouted angrily. I walked over to the edge of the track and directed Pete to the infield. He looked bewildered but turned the car into the infield and brought it to a stop near the trailer. Frank reached through the window and turned off the engine.

The front of the car was heavily damaged, but the engine seemed unharmed. And all four tires were pointed in the correct direction, which was a good thing. But steam spewed from the radiator and seeped from beneath the edges of the hood. A stream of liquid dribbled from the bottom.

On the track, a crew with a tow truck had hooked onto the car that Pete hit and was dragging it out of the way. I thought we might escape without any further repercussions until I saw the driver of the damaged car headed in our direction. An older guy with a barrel chest and thick, muscular arms. His face was red with anger, and he walked with determination. Head tilted forward, arms pumping in time with each step.

Pete was climbing from the car when the driver reached

us. "You wrecked me on purpose!" he shouted, jabbing Pete in the chest to emphasize each word.

"You were going too slow," Pete countered.

"I was supposed to be going slow," the man retorted, leaning closer, his nose almost touching Pete's. "We were under caution, dumbass. Didn't you see the flag? Didn't you see the lights?"

Pete looked bewildered. I forced my way between them. "This was my fault," I said.

The driver frowned. "What do you mean?"

"I put him out there without telling him what the flags meant."

"Well then maybe I should kick your ass instead," he roared.

Men from a neighboring crew took him by the arms and coaxed him away. As they led him aside, the head steward arrived. He wasn't pleased but seemed sympathetic. "Look," he said, "I understand what you're trying to do here, but we have a race to run and other competitors to protect."

"Right," I said.

"If you want to keep racing," he continued, "your driver will have to learn the rules."

"I understand."

"Your car will be scored last tonight, which normally would give you one point toward the track championship, but I'm gonna have to penalize your team."

"What kind of penalty?"

"I'll only dock you the one point you would have received, but if this happens again, I'll have to do more."

As the steward walked away, I glanced toward the track and saw George talking to the angry driver. George seemed to know everyone, and I hoped he could help us avoid any further trouble. Saturday night tracks were notoriously confrontational—on the track and in the infield. I didn't want any trouble when we came back the following week, assuming we could get the car repaired.

Leaving the infield required us to cross the track, but with cars on the track waiting to finish the Bomber race, and more races yet to come that night, leaving immediately was impossible. We were forced to stay where we were until the last race finished. While we waited, I found a concession stand in the third turn and bought everyone a hotdog and soft drink. We ate at the truck and watched the other classes run their events.

It was late when we arrived at the farm, well past midnight. We unloaded the car in front of the shop and dropped the trailer beside the building. The guys were tired and dejected. As they started toward the house, a car crested the hill and came to a stop at the shop. The driver's door opened, and the driver stepped out. I recognized him immediately as the driver who had confronted us at the track.

George tried to intervene. "Gene, maybe this isn't the time for this."

Gene ignored him. "Where's the driver of that car?" he demanded.

I stepped in. "You'll have to deal with me. This was my idea."

"Your idea wrecked my car."

"I'm sorry about that. Our driver made a mistake."

Gene glanced around at the guys. "You really got drug addicts up here?"

"Ex-addicts," I said.

Pete joined us. "I'm the driver," he said.

"You don't look like no drug addict."

"I'm not," Pete replied. "I'm an ex-addict."

"You don't look like a race car driver, either."

"I could say the same for you."

Gene's jaw flexed and I thought we were about to have a fight, but before I could intervene, he laughed. "You might make it yet," he said. He looked past us and pointed to the car. "Y'all built this car yourself?"

"Yes," I replied.

"Not a bad-looking machine." He walked around the car and seemed to relax. When he reached the other side, he paused as if thinking about something, then he pointed to me and said, "Have this car and your boys at the track Monday morning. Eight o'clock." He didn't wait for a reply but got into his car and drove away.

When he was gone, I looked over at George. "Who was that?"

"Gene Tapia," George said. "He's been racing around here a long time. Serious about it. Owns a car in every class."

"Explains why he was so upset."

"Yeah."

"Well," I said to the guys, "if we're going to take this car to the track on Monday, we'll need to work on it tomorrow afternoon."

"Even though it's Sunday?" someone asked.

"Yes," I answered. "Even though it's Sunday. We'll go to Mass in the morning and work on the car in the afternoon."

"And what about the fieldwork?" Frank asked. "Can we miss that on Monday?"

George spoke up. "I'll talk to Lewis. I think we can get by on our own for a day."

On Sunday morning, David and I attended Mass with the guys in Alexandria. After lunch, we went to the shop where everyone was waiting.

"There's a lot of work to do," I said, "but what do we do first?"

"Wash it," Rick said.

They pushed the car to the concrete pad near the fence-row where Pete was waiting with the power washer connected and ready. He and Reuben took turns cleaning the car, then we rolled it back to the shop and removed the radiator. It was damaged beyond repair, so we removed one from the truck we'd brought up from the field months before, then tested it to make sure it didn't leak.

The front frame of the car required straightening and the radiator brackets had to be altered to accommodate the one we'd salvaged from the truck. Doing that required measuring, bending, and welding. Thankfully, George arrived to help. It was late in the afternoon when we finally had the radiator in place and connected. We filled it with coolant, started the engine, and let it run until it reached operating temperature. Everything held together without leaks.

When all of that was done, we used string and a measuring tape to check the alignment of the wheels. As I expected, the wheels were not pointed in the correct direction. Correcting that required several adjustments to the front suspension to bring the wheels into alignment with each other and the car.

Early Monday morning, we once again hitched the trailer to the truck, loaded the car onto it, and started toward the racetrack. Tommy, the new group leader, brought most of the guys in the farm's van. David, Fred, and Pete rode with me in the truck.

When we arrived at the track, the parking lot was empty but the gate that led onto the infield was open. We drove inside and parked on the grass near the place where the cars lined up for qualifying. A few minutes later, Gene arrived and parked next to us. "Get the car unloaded," he said, not bothering with a greeting.

We pushed the car off the trailer and Gene began explaining the sport of auto racing to the guys. Then he talked about how an automobile race worked, the color of the flags the flagman used to manage the race, and the lights positioned around the track with colors that matched the flags. "They're just like the traffic signals on the highway," he said. "Green means go. Yellow means slow down. Red means stop." After that, he talked about how a race ends. What to do when you lose. What to do when you win.

"Now," he said, finally, "let's see how you handle the car. Where's that driver that hit me?" Pete stepped forward. Gene pointed to him. "Get in the car."

Pete climbed in behind the steering wheel and strapped himself into the safety harness. Gene leaned through the window. "You see that pedal on the right?"

"Yes," Pete replied.

"That's the gas pedal. See the one on the far left?"

Pete nodded.

"That's the clutch. Use it when you shift gears. And the one in the middle is the brake pedal. When you come up behind someone during a race or when we're under caution, put your foot on that middle pedal to slow down the car." He smiled. "Do you remember which color is for caution?"

"Yellow," Pete said.

"If you run up on somebody, especially when we're under caution, take your foot off the gas and put it over on the brake."

Pete had a sarcastic tone. "Would I ever brake the car any other time?"

"Actually, yes, smart guy," Gene said. "You can use the brake to help the car get through the curves, but if you do that, you use your left foot on the brake and keep your right foot on the gas. You don't want the engine to slow down at all. Got it?"

Pete nodded. "Sort of."

"Okay. We'll figure that part out as we go," Gene said. "Take the car around for a lap or two and let me see what you can do."

When Pete completed his laps, Gene gave him some pointers on how to improve, then Frank took a turn. Then Reuben. Then Gary. And on through the rest of the group. I thought we would only be there for the morning, but we spent the entire day at the track, driving the car and listening to Gene talk about racing.

Each of the guys took multiple turns, including David, after which Gene gave them tips, suggestions, criticisms, and welcome words of encouragement. Everyone had fun, and all of them learned more about cars and racing than they ever imagined possible, but by afternoon, Pete and Frank emerged as the fastest and the ones with the most skill in handling the car.

On the final cycle of laps, Frank was the last to go. As he wheeled the car around the track for the final time, Gene checked his watch, then looked over at me and grinned. "That kid is good."

"How fast was he?"

Gene turned the watch so I could see but I had no idea what it meant. "How good is that?" I asked.

"Fast enough to qualify that car with the Late Models," Gene replied.

"He must be getting all the speed it has."

Gene grinned. "He's got the talent for it."

I was proud of him, especially since he seemed to have fun with the car, but the thought of it made me smile. Of all the things Lewis hoped to accomplish with the program, I was certain discovering racing skills wasn't one of them.

CHAPTER 19

On Tuesday evening, I left David at home and went to Alexandria to have dinner with Susan. I had called her Sunday to arrange it, thinking if she was at the track for the race, maybe she really was interested. It felt awkward going on a date in a pickup truck, wearing a sport coat, and being with a woman other than Julia, but I wanted to see her.

We ate at The Odeon, a restaurant in downtown Alexandria that George told me about, though after seeing the menu and the prices, I doubted he'd ever eaten there. Over dinner, we talked about many things. My past—some of it. Her past—a lot more than mine. She grew up in Lafayette, attended Tulane University, and taught school. After teaching for a few years, she went back to school for a master's degree and became a counselor. She'd been in several serious relationships but never married. Both parents were still alive. And she had a sister who lived in Houston. I didn't tell her that much about me.

When we left the restaurant, I noticed a car parked at the curb in the next block. The driver seemed to be watching us and making no attempt to hide that fact from anyone. As we drove away, he came behind us.

Susan was talking about something, but I wasn't paying any attention to what she said. My eyes kept darting between the street in front of us and the image of the car behind us in the rearview mirror. Finally, she noticed I was distracted and said, "What's the matter?"

"That guy behind us is following us," I replied. She turned to look but I reached over with my hand and stopped her. "Don't," I said. "Just watch the car in the side mirror."

At the next corner, I made a last-second turn onto the cross street. The force of the turn caught Susan off-guard and slung her against the door. Her shoulder banged against the glass. "What are you doing?" she complained. I didn't answer her. The car behind us made the corner as quickly as we did. I concentrated on what to do next.

A few seconds later, we came to another corner, and I repeated the maneuver. This time, though, the corner had a traffic signal and I timed it so that the light was red when I made the turn. The car following us ran the light, dodging cross traffic, in an effort to keep up.

Two blocks later, I'd had enough. I jammed on the brakes, stopping the truck in the middle of the street, then I threw open the door and jumped out to face the driver behind us. My sudden appearance, right there in the street, feet apart, fists balled at my side, caught him unprepared. His eyes were wide as he swerved wildly to miss me and then sped away.

When I got back in the truck, I saw Susan was upset. "What is going on?" she asked, this time demanding. "Why was he following us?"

"I don't know," I replied.

"Why would someone be doing that?"

"You remember what I told you about New Orleans?" In telling her about myself, I told her the part about living on the street and about the night Pump was killed.

"You think the guy in the car has something to do with that?"

"I think he could," I replied. "But whatever he's up to, it can't be good."

With the car no longer behind us, I relaxed some, but only a little, and drove a circuitous route to Susan's house, to make sure no one else was following. Rather than trying to allay her worry with empty reassurance, I used the time to tell her about my past in greater detail. If she and I were going to continue seeing each other, and if our relationship had any hope of developing into something more, she needed to know who I really was and what I had been through.

When we reached her house, I parked in the driveway and walked with her to the front door. It was another awkward moment for me. Do I kiss her goodnight? Do I play it safe? Reading the nonverbal cues of a dating companion was more difficult than I remembered it being. I don't know if she sensed how I was feeling or if she was shaken by the guy in the car, but when we reached the front door, she touched my forearm and said, "Would you mind coming inside with me? I'm a little worried."

"Sure," I said. "Let me take a look around." I focused on her as I spoke, searching for a hint, a sign, a light in her eyes to tell me what she meant—come inside and say a while, come inside and kiss me—but I saw nothing and assumed she really meant only what she said.

She remained near the front door while I checked the kitchen and utility room, then down the hall past the bedrooms and the bath, before coming back to the front room. "It looks good," I announced.

"Thanks," she replied, with a genuine sense of relief.

I said goodnight and turned for the door, determined not to take advantage of the moment, but she took my arm to stop me, and we kissed. Her lips were soft, and I enjoyed the feel of them against my own, so I kissed her again.

On Wednesday morning, David and I left the cottage as usual and went to Mass in Alexandria with Frank. When the service ended and we came outside to walk back to the truck, I saw a car parked at the next corner. It looked like the same car that had followed Susan and me the night before. I thought about confronting the driver to find out why he was there, then remembered David and Frank were with me and thought better of it. No need in putting them in any greater danger than they might already be in.

We made it to the truck without incident, but I noticed the driver made no attempt to hide the fact that he was watching us. As we drove away, I watched the car in the rearview mirror. It followed us to the highway but instead of turning north, as we did, it turned south. No one else seemed to take its place and the road was clear behind us all the way back.

When we arrived at the farm, I dropped David at the farmhouse to study with Jessica, then took Frank to the barn where he joined the others from the group. They went to the field with George to catch up on the work they missed Saturday when we went to the race and for the time they spent with Gene at the track on Monday.

With everyone doing something else, the barn and shop were deserted. Lewis was alone in his office. I expected him to come over and confront me about all that had happened at the track, and about racing taking the guys away from the farm tasks they normally would have covered, but he never showed. And if he wasn't coming to see me, I wasn't about to go see him.

That night, David and I ate dinner at the cottage. As we were clearing the table, I heard a noise from the front porch, like the sound of footsteps. I moved to the window and glanced out from the edge of the curtains. A man was standing near the front door. I yelled at him through the windowpane, and he ran away.

David came to where I was. "Who are you yelling at?"

"Some guy on the porch," I replied.

He lifted the edge of the curtain and looked out. "I don't see anyone."

"He ran off."

"Who was it?"

"I don't know."

"Think it was that guy in the car we saw this morning?"

"Could be." I tousled his hair playfully, hoping to lighten the mood. "Don't worry about it. Probably nothing." I started toward the television. "Let's play a video game.

The next morning, when we came out to go to the farm, we saw footprints on the front porch and tire tracks in the dirt on the road to the barn. David looked concerned. "What's this about, Dad?"

"Nothing," I replied.

"It's not nothing," he responded. "So, you might as well tell me."

I'd been reluctant to talk to David about my past for fear it would taint his view of me and prevent us from having any relationship at all. Now, having come quite far in our understanding of each other and in our affection for each other, I thought he might blame me for bringing the troubles of my past into his own present. But, with people showing up at the house and peeking through the windows, there seemed no way to avoid talking about it.

"When you were living with your mother," I began, "and I wasn't there, did she tell you where I was?"

"When I was little, she used to tell me you were sick and you had gone away because of it."

"But you knew that wasn't true, right?"

"At first I believed her, but as I got older, I knew she wasn't being straight with me." He looked over at me. "You were living on the street, weren't you?"

I nodded. "Who told you?"

"Grandma. I overheard her talking about you to someone and started asking questions."

"I was a drunk," I said. "And that—"

"You were an alcoholic?"

"I am an alcoholic."

"But I thought you got over it."

"You never get over it," I replied. "You just get better at living with it."

"Do you still want to drink?"

"Yes," I said. "Sometimes." I hadn't thought about it much since coming to the farm but admitting even that much made me uncomfortable. Still, he needed to know, and I needed to tell him. "Back then," I continued, "I was living on the street in the French Quarter."

"On the street. As in, really on the street?"

I nodded. "Sleeping on park benches. Benches at the

bus stop. A doorway. Wherever I could a spot find that seemed safe."

"You were homeless?"

"Yeah."

"Why didn't you just come stay with us?"

"Your grandmother and grandfather never wanted me around when I was sober," I said. "They certainly didn't want me around when I was drinking."

"But they would have let you stay there. I mean, you could have slept … in the garage."

"Later, when I did get off the street, I lived at the church near their house."

"St. Dominic's," he said. "I remember seeing you there, once or twice."

"You were young. Did you even know who I was?"

"Grandpa told me."

I hadn't known that David had seen me, or that Julia's father had told him who I was, and hearing that her father had pointed me out made me think I might have underestimated him after all. "I'm sorry about all of that," I said.

"All of what?"

"Me on the street. Drunk all the time when I should have been with you."

"It's okay," he said. "But what does this have to do with people following us and coming around the house at night?"

"While I was living on the street, I saw someone shoot somebody. Actually," I said, correcting myself, "I saw a man get shot. I didn't get a very good look at the shooter."

"Did you know the guy who got shot?"

"Yeah," I said. "I knew him."

"Did he die?"

"Right there on the street," I replied.

"Wow." David sighed. "That's pretty bad."

"Yeah."

"Is that why that detective has been coming around?"

I glanced in his direction. "You know about that?"

"Everyone knows about it. He came to the barn in broad daylight. All the guys in the group were standing right there."

"Who told you?"

"They were all talking about it."

"Well keep your eyes open," I said. "If they were bold enough to come to the house, and come up on the porch, there's no telling what they might do next."

CHAPTER 20

Throughout the day on Wednesday, everything went as usual and I was beginning to think that trouble might have passed us by, but late that night I was awakened by the sound of breaking glass and the heavy thud of footsteps on the living room floor. I rolled out of bed and landed on my hands and knees, then, still crouching, I reached for my pants. I stood to put them on and stumbled to the corner of the room, caught myself against the wall, and fastened the pants around my waist.

Suddenly, the bedroom door flew open, and three blasts roared from the barrel of a shotgun. Flames from the shots flashed across the room in quick bursts. Lead shredded the mattress and pillow. Splinters flew from the headboard.

The gunman racked another cartridge into the chamber, but before he could shoot again, I charged from the corner of the room, struck him with my shoulder, and drove him backward toward the doorway. He bounced off the doorjamb hard and groaned with pain but before he could recover, I hit him in the gut as hard as I could, and he slid to the floor.

My only thought was of David and whether he was all right, so I stepped over the intruder, determined to reach the hall. As I did, he caught my leg and I fell. I struggled to recover but the guy was on his feet and as I stood, he grabbed me from behind with an arm around my throat.

The door to David's room opened and he appeared in the hall, wide-eyed and alert. When he saw what was happening, he grabbed the guy by the hair and pulled him backward. The intruder elbowed David but as he turned back to face me, I struck him with a knee to the groin. He fell forward, landing on the floor where he curled in a fetal position, his hands instinctively clutching his crotch.

I grabbed David. "Are you okay?"

"Yeah," he said. "But who is that, and why is he——"

The shotgun went off right beside me, the heat of the blast singeing the hair on my arm. I was startled at first but as I looked down at my arm, I saw the guy on the floor holding the gun with both hands and trying to load another round. How he got the gun I don't know but I grabbed the end of the barrel and pointed it away from us as I stepped forward and stomped on his face with the heel of my foot. Then I stomped on him again and again until his body went limp, and the shotgun slipped from his grip.

Behind me, David was on the floor in a sitting position, his back against the wall, both hands pressed against his hip. I let go of the gun and dropped on my knees beside him. A dark red splotch covered his t-shirt. I lifted it and saw a gaping wound on his thigh.

"It hurts, Dad," he groaned.

I took a towel from the bathroom and placed it against his side. "Try to hold this in on it," I said.

"What are were going to do?"

"We have to get you out of here," I said. "You need a doctor."

"But what about him?" David asked, with a nod to the intruder.

"He'll have to fend for himself," I replied.

I returned to the bedroom and slipped on a pair of shoes, then hurried back toward David. As I came into the hall, the intruder slid his knees underneath his torso, as if to stand. I stomped on his head once more and felt it hit bounce against floor. He flopped to one side and lay motionless.

David was unable to walk so I picked him up and carried him through the house, cradled in my arms. At the front door I saw the frame had been split where the bolt on the lock had been kicked through it. Glass was broken from the top half. It crunched beneath my feet.

The pickup truck was about ten yards from the porch. I carried David to the passenger side and gently placed him on the seat, then ran to the driver's side and got in behind the steering wheel. Much to my relief, the engine started without any problem—I had been worried the intruder might have tampered with it—and we drove down the farm road toward the barn.

Before we'd gone far, headlights from an approaching vehicle appeared in front of us. "That's not good," I said.

David raised himself up to see over the dash. "Turn around," he said. "Go back by the house."

"By the house?" That didn't seem like a good idea.

"Just do it," he demanded. "I'll show you."

The other vehicle was getting closer, and I had no better idea, so I did as he said and turned the truck around. Seconds later, we were at the house. "What now?" I asked.

"Keep going," David said with a wave of his hand. "Go past the house."

Not far beyond the cottage, the road seemed to end in a wooded area of the pasture, and I was about to yell at him when David said, "Now, turn left."

The front wheels bounced over a log as we turned, and the headlights washed over woods to reveal a trail. "It's an old road," David explained.

"Where does it go?"

"Out to the one that leads to the highway, near where I get off the bus."

The trail was hardly a road, but I pressed the gas pedal anyway and the truck seemed to fly through the woods. In the mirror I saw the other vehicle was still behind us, but when I looked again, I saw it bounce to one side and the lights disappeared. David was propped against the seat, looking out the rear window. "I think they wrecked," he said.

"That's good," I responded. "But if the shooter at the

house came in his own car, they might get it and come after us."

David turned to face forward. "Then what do we do?"

"We keep going," I said. "You need help. How are you feeling?"

"It's not too bad," David said bravely, but his face was pale, and I could see he'd lost a lot of blood.

When we reached the highway, I turned left, and we sped past the road that led to the farm. Not long after that I saw headlights in the mirror from a car coming in our direction. I pressed the gas pedal to the floor and the truck sped even faster.

Minutes later, I glanced in the mirror and saw the car was gaining on us quickly. "Get down," I said, and I pushed David toward the floor of the cab. He groaned as he slid out of sight.

When the car was near our rear bumper, a shot rang out. I ducked as the back glass of the cab exploded. More shots came from the car. Bullets struck the tailgate of the truck and the side mirror, shattering it, but we kept going.

David looked up at me. "Dad, I think those guys mean to kill us."

Despite the circumstances, the comment struck me as humorous, and I chuckled. "I think you're right, David. They seem committed to the cause."

Our situation seemed grim but as we topped a hill, we met a police car coming toward us. I pressed my hand on the horn in a long, loud, continuous sound and saw the patrol car whip around in the middle of the highway. It started toward us, blue lights flashing, and the car that had been following us veered to the right onto a side road. The patrol car went after it.

The hospital in Alexandria was located downtown. We ran three traffic lights and slid to a stop at the emergency room entrance. An attendant came out to see what was going on. A nurse followed with a gurney. They put David on it and wheeled him away to a treatment room. I parked the truck and by the time I found them, they had David's clothes off and were checking his wound.

The trauma physician turned to me. "This injury came from a gunshot?"

"Yes," I said. "Someone broke into our house."

"We have to call the police."

"Good." I pointed to David's leg. "How bad is it?"

"This looks like a blast from a shotgun. Some of the pellets struck his hip and side. We can take care of those without much trouble. The worst part is the wound to the thigh. It appears to have reached the bone. We'll need to operate before we know more about that."

"You'll do that now?" I asked.

"Yes."

An assistant caught my eye and gestured toward the hall. "Come on," she said. "I'll take you to the waiting room. They'll have some questions for you to answer and forms to fill out. Someone will come to get you when your son is out of surgery."

A clerk met us in the hallway with a clipboard and admission forms. I filled in as many blanks as I could. When I finished, I used a pay phone and called Lewis to explain the situation, then I tried to reach Detective Aldrich, but he didn't answer.

As I hung up the phone, an Alexandria patrolman arrived, and I told him what happened. "Lovell Aldrich from the New Orleans police department knows about this case," I added. "He can fill you in on more details than I can." The patrolman seemed familiar with the situation, though I didn't ask how.

After the patrolman was gone, I sat alone with only my thoughts for company. The trouble we'd had with people following us and now the break-in at the house was all my fault. I hadn't done anything wrong to bring it on, but years earlier I had witnessed a murder, and I was there when it occurred because I was living on the street—a drunk looking for a handout so I could stay drunk. Numb to my surroundings, to myself, to the thoughts that filled my head when I was sober. Parents who cared little for me. In-laws who cared even less. A wife too disgusted with me to share the same residence. A son I had abandoned. Guilt and shame rose inside me as the memories kept coming and coming. Things I could have done. Things I should have done. And things I never did.

Very quickly, the walls of the hospital waiting room closed in on me and I felt myself begin to fragment. Part of me slipping into the blackened depths of a deep dark sea, the other part unable to keep me from going. Down, down, down to the bottom with no way for anyone to know where I was or even think of coming to find me.

Then the door from the outside opened and I saw Susan coming toward me. I must have looked desperate because when our eyes met, she rushed in my direction. Before I could stand, she was on the seat beside me, and I felt her arms around my neck. Relief swept over me, and I buried my face against the base of her neck, inhaling the sweet fragrance of her perfume, and with every breath the blackness that had surrounded me evaporated. My sense of self returned, and I felt whole again.

After a moment I raised my head, and she kissed me gently on the lips. "How did you find me?" I asked.

"Jessica called me."

"How did she know?"

"Mike told her."

I pulled away and sat up straight in the chair with my hand gripping hers. "How did he know?" I asked.

"The police are all over the farm," she said.

"Did they find the guy who broke into the house?"

"I'm not sure."

"When we left, he was lying on the floor in the hall."

"They said there was blood." She put her arm through mine and leaned her head against my shoulder. "This is what you worried would happen."

"Yeah," I said. "This is it."

An hour later, Lewis arrived. "I just came from your house," he said. "Deputies are there. City police. An investigator from the state police. They've been over the property."

"What about Aldrich?"

"They said he had been there, but he was gone by the time I arrived."

We were still talking when Aldrich entered the waiting room. He gestured for me, and I followed him up the hallway, away from the others. When we were out of their hearing he said, "We got the guy from your house."

"What about the ones who chased us?" I was sure there was more than one person in the car.

"Deputies caught them in Winnfield."

"Who were they?" I asked.

"Some guys out of New Orleans." He gave me a look. "You should be thankful you came through this in one piece."

"I am."

"Those guys meant to kill you and they weren't fooling around."

"I know."

"Do you have some place to stay?"

"I can sleep at the house, but I imagine I'll be down here at least tonight."

He shook his head. "You can't get back in the house until they finish working the scene."

"Okay."

"I know this is a bad time to talk," he continued, "but we'll have to go over this soon. This case has gotten a little bigger than when we talked before."

"Do we need to talk now?"

"No. I'll catch up with you. Just take care of your son and we'll talk later."

"Does he need a guard on the room?"

"I've alerted hospital security and the nursing staff. I think he'll be okay."

David spent several hours in surgery that night and when they took him to a room, he was on heavy doses of pain medication. He slept the remainder of the night and through most of Thursday, too. I stayed with him in his room, seated in a chair beside the bed, but I was unable to slow my mind or divert it from the details of my past, replaying, again and again, the path my life had taken, the choices I had made, and the consequences those choices had visited on Julia and now on David.

Perhaps Julia's pregnancy was the result of both our

choices, but drinking had been solely my own doing, as was the choice to live on the street. After Julia left, I could have continued to work and pay the bills. Nothing compelled me by force to get drunk. And even when I was out of money, I could have returned to my parents, admitted defeat, and lived with them at least for a while. If nothing else, they would have let me sleep in the garage. Instead, I chose the street. That's how I came to know Pump and Eddie. And that's how the guy ended up in our house with a shotgun. And how David got shot. And how he came to be in the hospital bed next to me.

Early Friday morning, David awakened and ate breakfast. We talked about his condition and events of the break-in, but around mid-morning he drifted off to sleep again. I dozed, too, having finally worked enough memories through my mind to find a measure of peace.

Sometime later that day, I felt David squeeze my hand. My eyes opened and I looked over at him. He smiled and said, "Was the guy at the house the one you were talking about?"

"From the street?"

"Yeah."

"He wasn't the one who killed Pump," I replied.

"That guy was trying to kill you."

"Yes," I said. "I think he came for both of us." I felt immediately I shouldn't have said that, not to a kid his age, but I wanted him to know the threat was real.

"Think he'll come back?"

"Not that guy. Or the ones behind us in the car. The police caught them."

"Think whoever's behind it will send someone else?"

"I hope not."

We were silent for a while, and I checked to see if he was still awake. He was staring up at the ceiling as if in thought. It was a lot for anyone to process, but especially for a kid his age. An intruder at the house. Shooting at us. And us fighting for our lives. And then getting shot. I wondered if he needed a counselor and thought of Susan, but if she and I were involved romantically, she might not be the best person for him to talk to. In the past, before we knew enough to consider professional counseling, parents worked out things like this for themselves. Maybe I could—

David pushed himself higher in the bed and looked at me, his eyes alert. "What day is it?" He sounded concerned and he had a serious frown.

"Friday," I said.

He glanced out the window. "Friday morning?"

"Yes. Why?"

"Is the car ready?"

"The car?" I was puzzled. "What car?"

"The race car," he said. "Tomorrow's Saturday. We have a race at the track."

I hadn't thought about the car or racing since the night of the break-in, but it wasn't something I was concerned about right then. "You won't be racing for a while," I replied with a dismissive gesture.

"Maybe not," he said, "but the guys will."

"They'll be—"

"They can't wait for me to get well," he said, cutting me off.

"There'll be other days at the track." I heard the words come from my mouth in a parental tone that sounded remarkably like my father. It bothered me that I sounded that way, but it seemed like a good thing to say. A good attitude to have. There were other things more important than cars and racing.

"You aren't taking them?" The pitch of his voice was higher.

"No."

"You can't do that." He was angry and insistent. "They've worked hard on that car. They can't miss a single race. The season isn't that long."

"You're not going and I'm not—"

"Yes, you are," David insisted. "You have to go. You have to take them. They're counting on you."

"I'm staying right here. I'm not leaving you here alone."

"Dad, I'll be fine," he argued. "You have to go. They can't do it without you and if we miss a race, we'll lose any shot we have at the track championship." When I didn't respond immediately, he said, "You're going. And that's all there is to it."

Hearing that, I couldn't help grinning, not at the substance of what he'd said, but at the familiarity of our interaction. We were learning we could talk to each other about anything, and I liked that. "But you shouldn't be here alone," I said.

"Then call Susan." A phone was on the stand beside the bed, and he pointed to it. "Call her and ask her to sit with me."

That pleased me, too—that he was comfortable enough with her and with our relationship to suggest her. So, I picked up the phone and dialed her number.

CHAPTER 21

Susan agreed to sit with David at the hospital Saturday night while George and I took the car and guys to the track. It was Frank's turn to drive. He qualified the car well. Someone suggested he might have benefited from running slower to get a starting spot near the front. "And if you do that," Frank reminded them, "you'll probably get thrown out for sandbagging."

"None of that matters now," I said.

"Why not?" Rick asked.

"Frank was the fastest car tonight."

"Really?" Frank grinned. "I was the fastest?"

"Yeah," I replied. "You're starting last."

When the cars lined up for the race, Frank was next to Gene Tapia. Even from a distance, I could see the smile on Gene's face. He was as proud of the guys as I was.

The flagman waved the green flag, and the cars came up to speed. They were side-by-side through the first turn, then Frank picked up two places on the backstretch. He took three more places on the next lap. Two laps later, there was a wreck and the cars made three laps under caution while the damage was removed from the track. Four laps after the race resumed, Frank took the lead. No one challenged him as he cruised to our first win. The guys were ecstatic. I could hardly believe it. We ran out to the track to congratulate him and crowded around the car when the flagman presented the trophy. George and I were in tears.

Afterward, as we loaded the car onto the trailer, a track steward appeared. He had a grim expression. "We have a challenge," he said.

My heart sank. "For what?"

"Someone thinks your engine is illegal."

"What does that mean?" I asked.

"We need to check the position of the engine in the car, then we need to check the displacement of the cylinders," he said. "And we usually look at the carburetor, and the camshaft." He grimaced. "Can you go that deep in the engine where it sits?"

"Yeah," I said. "But we'll need to push it off the trailer so we can get to it."

The guys rolled the car off the trailer and raised the hood. A second steward arrived, and they measured the position of the engine on the frame. That was correct.

Rick removed the sparkplugs, and the steward inserted a device to measure the volume of each cylinder. A crowd gathered to watch, which made me uneasy. I was about to say something when Gene Tapia elbowed his way to the front. "Make sure you allow for the temperature, Earl," he said to the steward. "That engine is hot. You've got to figure that in."

The steward responded without looking up. "I know what I'm doing, Gene."

With Gene on our side, I turned to the steward. "You can't do it like this. I'm not showing what we have to a crowd."

The steward who was assisting with the inspection cleared the crowd away, except for the driver who protested, then they turned to the carburetor. Gary removed the breather and unbolted the carburetor, then handed it to the steward. He inspected it, and took some measurements, then handed it back. "That looks good," he said. "Let's see the camshaft."

We removed the radiator and the water pump, then the timing chain cover and the chain. That took a while because we had to use a gear puller to slide the chain sprockets off the shafts. While some of us did that, Gary and Pete removed the valve covers and took out the rods, so they didn't jam against the lobes on the camshaft. When that was done, they used a magnetic device to remove the lifters.

All of that took about an hour and finally, we slid the camshaft from the engine block. Someone brought a dial micrometer to measure the shaft's diameter and the width of the lobes.

Frank objected. "Not with that," he said.

The steward frowned. "Why not?"

"You'll scratch the surface."

"Then what do you suggest?"

Pete brought a digital device from the toolbox. "Use this," he said.

The protester spoke up. "How do we know it's accurate?"

"Measure something with yours," Frank said to the steward. "And then do it with ours."

The steward smiled. "That sounds like a good idea."

They did as Frank suggested and after comparing the readings, the steward was satisfied our device was accurate. He used it to check the camshaft, consulted a reference book to determine if the readings agreed with the manufacturer's specifications, then handed Pete the shaft. "It's legal," he said.

The protester was dissatisfied but left. The guys turned to me. "What do we do now?" The engine was in pieces.

"Put the covers on the heads," I said. "Bolt the water pump cover on the front. Wrap the lifters and pushrods in a rag and put them in the toolbox. Lay the camshaft in the cab of the truck. We'll put the engine back together at the shop."

Rick looked worried. "Will it be all right?"

"It'll be fine," I said. "You guys have already done this once."

They seemed to relax. "Yeah," Gary said. "We took this engine down to nothing, then put it back together."

"And it ran," Reuben said.

Everyone laughed.

"It ran," Reuben repeated, "and we won the race tonight." And the celebration started all over again.

It was late when we left the track and even later when we arrived at the farm. The guys pushed the car into the shop and put the extra parts on the workbench. I dropped the trailer by the fencerow, then drove to the hospital to see about David. Aldrich was waiting for me when I reached the hospital parking lot.

"You took your time about getting here," he said.

"I didn't know we were meeting," I replied.

"You know why I'm here?" He seemed aggravated. I didn't care for his tone.

"Not a clue," I said as I made my way toward the hospital entrance. "Something to do with the case, I guess." He was beside me still, so I asked, "What do you need?"

"Honesty," he said.

"You think I haven't been honest with you?"

"You haven't told me the truth."

I stopped abruptly and turned to face him. "You think I'm lying about something?"

He had a smartass grin. "We know about you and Eddie Morrisette."

Me and Eddie Morrisette…. He didn't know about me and Eddie. He thought he knew about me and Eddie.

My relationship with Eddie was one of convenience. I knew stuff about Eddie. Eddie knew stuff about me. That's the way it worked on the street, for those who stayed alive.

Everyone tried to keep things balanced. To maintain the status quo. Eddie was a distributor. He knew things about his supplier and about his dealers. That's how he kept things even. They knew things about each other. I wasn't one of Eddie's suppliers, but Pump was, and Pump used me to help keep an eye on his business. As a result, I knew things about Pump, and Eddie, and Eddie's supplier, things I wasn't necessarily supposed to know but knowing it kept me in an even position.

"Why didn't you tell me you knew him?" Aldrich asked. "Better yet, why did you tell me you didn't know him?"

"Everything I told you was the truth," I said. "I left out the part about Eddie because I didn't want him to find out I talked."

"You knew that was his car when you saw it in the street that night."

"Yeah."

"And you knew it when you saw that photo I showed you, back when we first met."

"Yeah."

Aldrich took me by the arm. "I got people back in New Orleans who are wondering just how uninvolved you really were with him."

I shrugged free of his grasp. "What does that mean?"

"I'll tell you what it means." He jabbed me with his index finger for emphasis. "It means you're going to meet with Eddie and get him to talk."

My heart sank. "You want me to wear a wire?" Wearing a wire to a meeting with Eddie was more of a risk than a guy like Aldrich could appreciate.

"Yeah," he said. "I do. And you know something else? You're gonna do it."

The only response was to try and put him off. "I'd be happy to help," I replied. "But I don't know where he is."

"That won't be a problem." Aldrich smiled. "He'll find you."

The following day Aldrich came to the hospital and told me Eddie had been seen in Alexandria. Then he took me down the hall to a treatment room where he fitted me with a wire—a listening device that allowed him to monitor my conversation. When it was in place he said, "Go home and wait. Eddie will be around to see you soon."

"How soon?"

"Soon enough," he said.

"You talked to him?"

"No. But I've been trailing this guy for a long time. I know how he operates. He didn't come all the way up here for nothing and he has no other reason to be here except for you."

"And my son."

"We have that covered."

"I need to be with David," I replied.

"Your girlfriend will stay with him."

I frowned. "My girlfriend?"

"That lady you were with the other day. Susan something-or-other."

"If Eddie's in town, I don't want to leave her and David alone."

"They won't be alone," Aldrich replied. "I got someone coming to help."

As Aldrich suggested, Susan came to stay with David. A female officer from the Alexandria police department joined them. I still didn't want to leave them but knowing an officer was there made it easier. And maybe if I helped Aldrich by meeting with Eddie, everyone would leave us alone. Maybe.

The drive back to the farm took half an hour. I parked in my usual spot near the front door of the cottage and got out. The first thing I noticed when I came from the truck was that the door of the house had been repaired. Whoever did the work did a great job. Except for the flecks of paint on the porch, it looked as if it had never been damaged.

Everything seemed fine but as I opened the door and went inside, I sensed something was wrong. When I looked across the room I saw why. Eddie Morrisette was seated in a chair near the sofa. His appearance in my house startled me.

"What are you doing here?" I asked.

"Jake," he replied with a grin. "Glad to see you still remember me."

"You're rather unforgettable, Eddie."

"I heard you been talking to Detective Aldrich. I hear you told him you didn't know me."

"That's not exactly what I said."

"Well, it's okay," Eddie said. "I'm not upset about it. In fact, it's rather reassuring."

"How's that?"

Eddie's expression turned serious. "It lets me know that you know what happens to snitches."

"Those goons you sent up here shot my son."

"I did not send them up here."

"Then who did?"

"I have partners now," Eddie replied. "I tried to tell them you were one of the good guys. That you and me been sharing secrets for a long time and you would never talk. But," he said with a shrug, "they ain't from New Orleans. They don't know how things work. I'm sorry that happened. They were supposed to be aiming for you, not the kid."

"And that's supposed to reassure me?"

"You know." He shrugged again. "I like you, but that's the cost of doing business."

"What do you want? Are you worried about Pump?"

"I'm not worried about no dead crackhead," Eddie scoffed. "Or the money." He frowned. "Is that what you think this is about?"

"If that's not it, then what's important enough for someone to want to kill me for it?"

"Come on, man." Eddie had a knowing look. "I gotta spell it out for you? Think, man. Think. What has made us best friends all these years?"

There were only two things I knew about him that… My eyes opened wide in a look of realization. "You and that prostitute?"

"She wasn't just any prostitute. She was Willie Crenshaw's sister, and he didn't like what she was doing. He already knifed three guys for being with her. That's why I made you a promise about what would happen to your wife if you talked. Only now, things have changed. I still got to do business with Willie, but your wife is dead. I lost my leverage with you."

And that's what I meant about keeping things balanced. I knew something about Eddie, but if I used it, he would do something to Julia. Those offsetting threats kept us balanced. Now that she was dead, he didn't have her to use against me.

"So, what does that mean?" I knew what it meant, but I wanted to hear it from him.

Eddie sighed. "It means I'm adding the whore and Pump to your tab. You keep your mouth shut about them and that boy of yours gonna be all right. You talk, I'll do to him what I promised to do to your wife."

"I ought to kill you right here."

Eddie laughed. "You ain't gonna kill me. We been friends too long for you to do that. Besides, I could cap you quicker than I capped Pump."

"Why did you kill him?"

"Ahh…you know." He seemed embarrassed. "It was just business."

"What kind of business?"

"I paid him with bogus bills. He got pinched for it. Said I owed him. That's what he was telling me that night on the street. I got mad. Put two in him without a second thought. Dropped him before he even knew what hit him. It was neat and clean, but I had a lapse. Drove away too quick. Forgot to pick up the money."

"Which I found."

Eddie nodded. "I came back to get it but by then, cops were everywhere. So, I had to let it go. I didn't know what happened to it until Aldrich started asking around. Somebody told me what he was saying. That's how I learned you was involved. After that, I just followed him and there you were. So, that's why I'm here. The whore and Pump, with your son as security, and we're cool."

Eddie stood as if he were going to shake my hand like we were closing a deal. I backed away from him, opened the front door, and stepped onto the porch. "Is that enough for you?" I asked in a loud voice.

Eddie was still staring at me when Aldrich appeared. "That's more than enough," he said as he moved past me.

Eddie glared at me. "You ratted me out."

"You threatened my son."

Aldrich placed Eddie in handcuffs. Patrolmen entered

the room and led him toward the door. He resisted when he got to me and leaned close. "That boy is dead." He grinned. "You think he's safe with that cop, but when I don't call at the appointed time, he's dead."

"You brought this on yourself," I snarled. "If you hadn't come looking for me, no one would have ever known anything. Now, they're going to learn it all."

A patrolman pushed him toward the door.

"I hope you said goodbye to your son," Eddie shouted.

Aldrich was in the room, and I turned to him. "What's he talking about?"

"That's just Eddie running his mouth."

"Are you sure David's all right?"

"Yeah," Aldrich said. "Why wouldn't he be?"

"Who chose the officer that's with him?"

"I don't know. I told them we needed someone, and she appeared."

"You don't even know if she's really a cop."

"You worry too much."

"He's my son!" I shouted. "Call the room."

Aldrich called the hospital room, but I could tell from the look on his face that no one answered. I didn't wait for him to explain but ran to the truck. "Wait," he shouted. "We need that wire." I ripped the device from my chest as I climbed into the cab of the truck and tossed it out the window as I sped away.

From the farm, I raced into town and slid the truck to a stop near the hospital entrance. I bounded up the steps and raced down the corridor to the elevator. I arrived at David's room to find his bed empty. A nurse entered the room behind me. "You just missed them," she said. "They were taking him down to X-ray."

"They?"

"An attendant with the wheelchair," she replied. "And the officer who'd been staying with him."

"Where is the woman?"

She had a questioning frown. "What woman?"

"The woman who was in here," I bellowed.

"I don't know." The nurse shrugged. "I didn't see her. Why are you—"

A muffled sound interrupted her. It seemed to be coming from the closet and as we stared at the door, I heard a loud thumping noise. I opened the closet door to find Susan stuffed inside. Her mouth was gagged with white medical tape that was wound around her head, and her hands were taped behind her back. I helped her from the closet and peeled away the tape.

"They have David," she gasped as she collapsed against me.

"They?" Panic hit me in the gut.

"That cop who was in here with us."

"Where were they taking him?" Waves of fear, worry and anxiety, washed over me.

"I don't know. But I don't think that cop is a cop. And she had someone with her."

"Who was it?"

"A guy," she said. "About your height but heavier. He had on a lab coat, but I don't think he worked for the hospital."

I took her by the hand. "Come on."

She resisted. "Where are we going?"

"To find David," I blurted.

"No." She shook her head vigorously, and I could see her eyes were wide with fright. "I can't," she said.

"You can't stay here," I argued. "And I have to go. So, come on." I pulled her toward the door. "We need to hurry." Reluctantly she came with me.

From the room, we ran up the hall to the nurses' station. The nurse working the desk glanced up as we appeared. "A man in a white lab coat came by here," I blurted. "A female police officer was with him. They were pushing a patient in a wheelchair. Did you see them?"

"Yes," the nurse said, nodding her head.

"Which way did they go?"

"They took the elevator." She pointed toward a bank of three elevator doors.

I pressed the elevator button, thinking we'd have to wait and maybe we should use the stairs, but the door for the first elevator opened. An empty wheelchair was inside. My heart sank at the sight of it, but I pulled Susan in with me and pressed the button for the ground floor. The doors closed and we started down.

The wheelchair was next to me, and I leaned down to look at it. Susan reached past me, pressed the ground floor button and the down arrow at the same time, and held them in place. "This makes it bypass the other floors," she said. I noticed she no longer looked scared.

We reached the first floor without stopping and rushed into the lobby. I glanced around, searching, checking, looking, desperate for anything that might provide a clue about where they had taken David. Nothing seemed obvious and I was on the verge of despair when I glanced out the door and saw a white lab coat lying in a flower bed near the walkway.

"This way," I said, and we ran out the door.

From the sidewalk, I scanned the parking lot and saw nothing at first, then I noticed a BMW at a traffic light across the way. It looked like Eddie's BMW, but it seemed ridiculous that they would be so obvious as to use his car. Still, having no other lead, I pointed in that direction and said, "That's them."

"Where?" Susan seemed bewildered. "I don't see them. Where are they?"

"That car at the light," I said and once again pulled her after me.

We ran to the truck and climbed into the cab, then sped across the parking lot and drove in the direction of the traffic signal where I'd seen the BMW. When we reached the street, I glanced at Susan. "Where does this road go?"

"Out to the highway," she replied. "This is the way you came in from the farm."

The light was red, and a line of cars waited for it, but with no time to waste, I bounced the truck over the curb onto the grass and drove by the waiting cars.

"Wrecking the truck won't help us," Susan said. She sat with one hand braced against the dash. The other gripped the armrest.

"If they go south on that highway," I said, "it'll take them to New Orleans."

"Eventually," she acknowledged. "But it's a long way from here to there."

At the corner, I caught an opening in traffic and turned the truck from the grass onto the pavement, then pressed the gas pedal to the floor and the truck roared down the street. We ran through five traffic signals without seeing the car.

"Maybe they turned off somewhere," I said. "Do any of those cross streets lead out of town?"

Susan didn't respond and I glanced at her, ready to shout for a response when I saw she was pointing out the front window. I looked in that direction and saw a patrol car parked on the shoulder, its blue lights flashing. The BMW was stopped in front of it.

"That's it," I said.

We slowed as we came alongside the car and through the

side window, I saw the woman from the hospital room in the driver's seat. David was seated in back.

"That's them," Susan said.

Car horns sounded behind us, but I ignored them and brought the truck to a stop in front of the BMW, blocking it from moving forward. As I came from the cab, the doors of the BMW flew open. The woman jumped from the driver's seat and a man came out on the passenger side. "Get the woman," I shouted to Susan as I hurried after the man.

From the street, the ground sloped sharply into a ditch with an embankment on the opposite side. The man from the car leaped across the ditch but slipped on the green grass of the embankment and slid to the bottom. I jumped in after him. He turned to fight me off, but I wrapped my arms around his chest and slung him around, banging his body against the embankment. His head bounced off the ground and his torso went limp. I pushed him across the ditch and put my knee against the center of his back to hold him in place. When I looked up toward the car, I saw Susan had the woman pinned against the fender. David was standing beside her, still in his hospital gown, grinning from ear to ear.

CHAPTER 22

Instead of going back to the hospital, I took David home with me. He was glad to be at the farm but didn't want to stay at the house by himself during the day. I didn't want him there alone, either, but I had work to do. So, I took him with me to the shop where he spent most of the day seated in a lawn chair near the door. The guys brought an electric fan to keep him cool and Frank brought him something cool to drink every few hours. David was weaker than he was willing to admit, but he seemed to enjoy the attention.

Despite the bravery Susan had shown earlier, she was deeply shaken by all that happened and apprehensive about staying at home alone, too. She spent the first night with a friend, then went to visit her sister in Houston. The distance from Alexandria seemed to assure her that she'd be safe there. On the day she left, I drove her to the airport and promised I'd be waiting when she returned.

We still had work to do on the farm and a race car to prepare for the next race. And David was right when he said the guys had worked hard. We'd all come a long way since we began, and I didn't want to let them down. They might not win a championship, but I didn't want to be the cause of it. Quite the opposite, my job—my calling, as I was discovering it—was to put them in the best position possible for achieving success. And I intended to do just that.

Our first task at the shop was to get the engine back together. Opening it at the track for the steward's inspection had exposed the internal parts to potentially devastating dust and dirt. By good mechanic standards, we should have disassembled it entirely and rebuilt it from the bottom up, but we didn't have time for that. All we could do was put it back together and hope it worked. The guys devoted every available minute to that effort and by the following Saturday, they had the engine reassembled and installed in the car. We went to the track hoping to complete the race with the engine still running and our championship dreams still alive. David went with us.

Our driver rotation schedule meant that week was Alan's turn to drive. He qualified second and finished third. The next Saturday, Rick drove. He bent a fender and finished second. The guys worked on the car and had it ready for Gary to drive the following weekend. They worked like that through the rest of the summer—farm tasks first, then every remaining minute devoted to the car—with driving duties rotated between them. They worked well together, and I was so proud of them I was about to burst.

With summer drawing to a close, and only a few races

left, we were back to Pete's turn as the driver. We arrived at the track and unloaded the car as usual. I expected Pete to climb into the car—he was always eager to take the track—but instead of getting behind the steering wheel, he gathered the guys and turned to me.

"We've been talking," he said. "David has been with us pretty much since the beginning and we think he needs a turn on the track."

"Yeah," Ron shouted. "Give the kid a shot at it."

The others were in agreement, and it was a kind gesture, but I wasn't sure it was the right thing to do. David hadn't fully recovered from his wounds, and he'd never driven the car in a race. That might not have been an issue earlier, but now that they were in contention for the championship it seemed important. Competition was close, very few points separated the top three cars. One misstep could make the difference between winning and not.

"I'm not sure about that," I said.

Frank spoke up. "He's been practicing in the pasture. I think he can handle it."

Pete smiled. "You're worried about the points."

"I'm worried about my son not being fully recovered yet," I replied.

Pete's smile broadened. "And the points," he said.

"Yes," I admitted. "I'm thinking about the points, too. For everyone."

"Isn't this car for us?" he asked.

"Yes."

"And isn't racing for us?"

"Yes."

"And isn't the championship for us?"

"What's your point?" I asked.

"If it's our car and our championship, why should you worry about the points?"

"He'll get us enough points," Reuben said. "Let him drive."

"Forget the points," Rick added. "Let the guy drive anyway."

David hadn't said anything, but I could see from the expression on his face that he really wanted to do it. And I could tell he was a little miffed at me for thinking he couldn't deliver a good finish. So, I handed him the helmet. The guys responded with a cheer, then helped him into the car.

With David driving, the car qualified in the middle of the pack. It was a tight race most of the night and he had to drive hard to get to the front. Along the way, he bent a front fender, then someone tapped him in the back and bent a rear fender, but as the race entered its final laps, he was running fifth. The guys were worried about the condition of the car. I was worried about David's lap times.

Frank noticed I was checking the stopwatch. "Is he close to breaking his time?"

"Real close," I said.

David finished in fourth place and brought the car to a

stop in the infield near the trailer. As he climbed from the car, a track steward approached me. "You gotta watch 'em on their qualifying times." He had an anguished look and he pointed to David. "That one was running really close on his."

"I know," I replied. "We were timing him."

"One of those laps just about went over the limit."

"I know."

The steward gestured to the guys. "I like what you're doing with these guys, but I can't cut you any slack on the rules."

"I understand."

The steward paused as he was leaving and gestured to the car. "That's a nice-looking car," he said. "I think having yours look so nice and run so well prompted some of the others to take better care of theirs."

That made me feel good about what we were doing. And it was true. Even the guys had noticed the improved appearance of the other cars from the way they looked at the first race.

On the way home, I glanced over at David. "You did good out there tonight."

"You didn't want me to drive, did you?"

"I was just worried about whether you'd recovered enough."

"I feel fine," he said. "Did you think I couldn't do it?"

"I wasn't sure."

"You thought I would wreck?"

"I don't know what I thought. There was just a lot going on—you are getting shot, the guys doing well. It was a conflicting moment for me. I'm sorry I didn't handle it better."

"That's okay."

"You drove a good race."

"That surprised you?"

"Well … actually … yes. It did surprise me."

"It surprised me, too," he said. "What was the steward talking about?"

"You were almost too fast," I said.

"Oh. That thing about not going faster than your qualifying time?"

"Yes. One or two of your laps were almost too fast."

David nodded. "I wondered about that. But they were about to run over me out there. I had to go faster to keep from getting hit."

I reached across the cab and tousled his hair. "You did great."

All through summer, the students had worked hard in the field and on the track with the car. It had been a grind, working in the heat and humidity, then in the shop, but the guys seemed to get through it without much trouble. Certainly nothing like the whining and complaining they'd shown when I first arrived.

The summer had been stressful for me, too. In addition to the heat and the work, and David getting shot, I missed seeing Susan. When she left, I thought she'd be gone for a week at most but when she didn't return, I phoned her. The conversation had been strained and cryptic, but I attributed it to her sister being present. Then a letter arrived and in it she mentioned she had been offered the possibility of a job. I wasn't sure what that meant—being offered the possibility of a job—but I hadn't argued with her about it. Having experienced the sometimes-tenuous nature of human relationships already, the last thing I wanted was to be with someone who didn't want to be with me. I assumed we were finished, even before we'd actually begun, and focused on the work at hand.

The guys also worked hard that summer on their classes with Jessica, preparing for the GED test. Some went so far as to take extra lessons to address areas where they felt particularly lacking—algebra and geometry chief among them. They were concerned they might not be ready for the test, especially Reuben, the oldest in the group, but I was encouraged by the subjects they chose to focus on. The tests weren't easy, but algebra and geometry still were elective classes in most Louisiana high schools. I doubted those subjects would be a big part of the exam. If those were the subjects the guys felt weak in—and if they really were competent in all the others—the test would pose no challenge for them at all.

Early in September, proctors arrived at the farm and over a two-day period administered the GED test in a battery of four examinations covering a range of subjects. It was tough for all of them and when it was over, the guys were exhausted. Most were certain they had failed. George and I found plenty of work to keep their minds diverted while they awaited the official results.

On a Saturday, three weeks later, we loaded the car for the short ride to the track for our next to last race. As the guys were fastening the car to the trailer, Lewis came from the office with eleven envelopes in his hand.

"These came today," he said, waving the envelopes to get everyone's attention. He laid them on the hood of the truck. "You've lived together, worked together, and studied together. And you took the exam together. Today, we're going to open these envelopes together and get the results. But whether you passed or failed, we're with you and we'll help you do whatever it takes to succeed."

As the guys opened their envelopes, the grins on their faces told us all we needed to know. They all passed, even Reuben, though he found it hard to believe.

He looked over at me and gestured with the letter. "Is this true?"

I pointed to the scoring boxes that showed the results for each subject. "They're all above the minimum," I noted. "And look right there." I tapped the bottom of the page where it said 'Congratulations.'

Reuben began to cry. The guys hugged him and wrestled him to the ground, then everyone piled on, shouting and laughing.

While they celebrated, Lewis came beside me. "Good to see them so happy."

"Yes," I said. "It is."

"We all played a part in making this happen, but I think you did more than most of us."

"I just tried to keep them engaged."

"And you did a great job at it," he said. "This car was your idea, and it really worked. I've never seen a group of guys so motivated and so transformed. You totally turned things around for them and for us."

It turned things around for me, too.

Although the GED result was a big deal, and in many ways the point of the program, we still had a race to run that night. And one more the following weekend. I pointed this out to the guys, and they gradually calmed down enough to finish loading the car for the ride to the track.

When we reached our place in the infield, Susan was there waiting. I was surprised to see her and gave her a hug. "Are you back for good?"

"Yes," she replied.

"I thought you would call. I would have met you at the airport."

"We should talk later," she said.

It seemed serious and I was apprehensive about what she might have to say, but I nodded and said, "Sure. After the race. Or tomorrow."

"Tomorrow might be better," she said.

Frank saw her and came to where we were standing. "Ms. Gilbert, I was wondering if you could help me with an application to LSU."

"You're thinking of applying?"

"Yes, ma'am. I have the application. I just need some help going through it."

I intervened. "They received the results from their GED examinations today," I said, by way of explanation.

Susan's eyes opened wide. "And you passed?"

"Yes, ma'am," Frank replied. "We all did."

"All of you?"

"Yes, ma'am."

She looked at me. "I've never heard of such a thing."

"They worked hard."

She gave Frank a hug. "I'm sure you did work hard," she said. "Congratulations."

"Thank you. Rick and Pete need some help with their papers, too."

She glanced at me again. "Papers?"

"Rick wants to attend McNeese State," I said. "Pete wants to apply to culinary school in New Orleans."

"Well of course I'll help you fill out the papers," Susan said. "And I'll give you a recommendation."

Frank beamed. "Great," he said. And I thought he was going to cry.

"You'll also need a letter from Jessica." Susan glanced at me again. "Is she still here?"

"She's still with the program," I replied. "But I haven't seen her tonight. Or Mike."

Susan raised an eyebrow. "Think they're absent together?"

"Might be. They've spent a lot of time together this summer."

Pete started the car and the sound of it drowned out our conversation. He let it run a moment, then backed it from its spot and drove toward the line of other cars waiting to qualify. Before I could get back to Susan, Gene Tapia appeared. I was surprised to see him. "I thought you'd be driving."

"Nah," he said. "I'm letting my son run it tonight. We can't win the points championship now and he'll be driving it next year anyway." He stood beside me with his arms folded in front, surveying the activity on the track. "You've done a great job with these guys."

"Thanks in no small part to your help," I noted.

"I just pushed you to the starting line," he replied. "You did the rest on your own."

"I don't think we'd be here without you."

"The car looks great."

"And so does everyone else's."

"That's just racing," he said with a dismissive gesture.

"What do you mean?"

"I mean, if you came out here with a green cigar box bolted on the hood of your car and won races, everyone would show up next week with a green cigar box bolted on their hood. You came with a great-looking car and ran well, so everyone else thought if they made theirs look better, maybe they'd run better too."

It was a compliment, actually. "Thanks," I said.

"We all needed to step up our effort," Gene said. "We just needed a push from you and your boys to get us moving."

As he walked away, I looked around for Susan, but she was gone. I wondered where she'd gone, but there wasn't time to worry about that right then. The pace car was leading the field onto the track. I climbed into the bed of the truck to watch.

Pete had qualified well and started from the back with the fastest cars. On the first lap, he passed two, and on the third he overtook two more. He kept going, picking up a spot in the running order on every lap and by the final lap he was in first place, but as he crossed the finish line and took the checkered flag, the engine quit, and a cloud of blue smoke came from beneath the car.

The guys were startled, and they all turned to me. "What was that?" they asked.

"The engine," I replied.

"What happened to it?"

"I don't know, but it's gone."

"Gone?" Reuben frowned. "You mean it fell out?"

"No," I answered. "It blew up."

"Will Pete be alright?"

"I didn't hear an explosion," Rick noted.

"It's just an expression," I explained. "Something inside broke."

Pete coasted partway back to the infield and the guys pushed him to the truck. Everyone was dejected. There was one more race in the season and the track championship for the division was within their grasp, but without an engine, we would be done.

They loaded the car onto the trailer, then we sat around and waited for the other classes to run their races. No one was interested in watching. I tried to interest them in a hot-dog, but they waved me off, opting instead to sit quietly on the trailer and in the bed of the truck.

Pete sat beside me. "Did I push it too hard?" he asked.

"You didn't do anything except drive a great race," I said.

"Then why did the engine quit like that?"

"Sometimes these things just happen. We'll take it apart and find out what's wrong, but parts in an engine are always under a lot of stress. Heating, cooling. Revving up. Slowing down. Sometimes they just break."

"Can we fix it?"

"We'll have to take it apart and see."

When the final race ended, we were the first crew to leave the track. No one in the truck said a word all the way back to the farm. George was behind us with the rest of the guys in his SUV. I was sure they were silent, too.

It was late when we parked in front of the shop. The guys dutifully unloaded the car, and I dropped the trailer by the fence. As I came back to the front, they were standing around the car, looking at it.

"Let's push it into the shop," I said. "It's late. You guys get a good night's sleep, and we'll start taking the engine apart tomorrow afternoon."

They were still standing there when Mike and Tommy, the counselors, arrived. "Let's go," Tommy said. "Get in the showers. You heard the man. It's late."

Pete and Reuben ignored him and pushed the car around the corner of the building toward the concrete pad where we washed equipment. Some of the others hurried to help. Tommy shouted. "What are you doing?" He sounded angry. "I said get to the house!"

By then, the car was out of sight on the opposite side of the building and as Tommy started in that direction, I heard the power washer start. Rick looked at me with a grin. "They're washing the car," he said.

"Sounds like it."

Tommy turned in our direction. "Washing the car? In the middle of the night?"

"Can't work on it until we get it washed," Rick said. He

moved around Tommy and ran toward the others.

Frank, who was halfway to the house, heard the noise and came at a run. Tommy yelled at him. "Where are you going?"

Frank ignored him and joined Rick on the far side of the shop. I started in that direction, too, and as I came around the corner, I saw the car on the concrete pad. Pete manned the power washer, spraying away dirt from under the frame. Reuben had a long-handled brush and was scrubbing the car body with soap. Rick and Frank kept the hoses straight and moved the bucket for Reuben. Ron and the others stood by, ready to help, but there wasn't much for them to do.

Tommy was angry over being ignored and he started toward them, but I grabbed his arm and held him back. "Let it go," I said.

"But I told them to hit the showers," he retorted. "They're supposed to do what I say."

"They've had a tough night."

"But it's late," he argued. "They need to stop."

"I'm not sure we could stop them even if we wanted to."

"They're supposed to do as they're told," he repeated.

"I know." I was still holding his arm and I used my grip to guide him in the opposite direction. "But look, this is exactly what we wanted them to do."

"What?" He had a heavy frown. "We want them to ignore a group leader and wash a car in the middle of the night?"

"Maybe," I replied. "We've been trying to get them to

take the initiative. Take responsibility. Do what needs to be done without being told."

Mike was there by then. "Is there a problem?"

"Yes," Tommy said. "They won't—"

"The engine blew," I said, interrupting Tommy and replying to Mike.

"They must be disappointed."

"They are, which is why they're over there washing the car."

Tommy pulled free of my grasp. "He thinks that's more important than doing what I told them to do."

Mike turned to him. "What did you tell them to do?"

"To take a shower and get to bed," Tommy shouted. "It's late."

I glanced in Mike's direction. "We missed you and Jessica tonight."

"Yeah," he replied. "Sorry about that."

There was more to the story, so I asked, "Is something wrong?"

Before he could respond, Tommy sighed heavily. "I'm going to the house. Y'all can deal with them on your own."

"Okay," Mike replied.

As Tommy walked away, I turned again to Mike. "What's up?"

He shoved his hands in his pockets. "Jessica wants us to get married."

"Congratulations," I said.

He looked away. "I just don't know."

"What do you mean?"

"It's a big step."

"Yes," I said. "It is. And with a baby. Someone else's baby."

"That's what I told her."

I grimaced. "I'm not sure you should have told her that."

"I know." He still wasn't looking at me. "She was pretty upset about it."

"You'll have to make your own decision, but if you marry her, you have to be ready to take the child, too."

"I know."

"It'll be a package deal," I continued. "You give yourself to Jessica. You give yourself to that baby. If you're in, you're all in."

He looked at me then and I could see the comment touched a nerve in an angry way. "Had a lot of experience with this sort of thing, have you?"

"I've had a lot of experience at messing things up," I said. "That's how I know what it will take to succeed."

Mike nodded. "I know," he conceded. "That's what I've been thinking about."

"It's a great privilege to be a dad. And in some ways, you've already had a taste of it with the guys."

"That's what she said."

The conversation between us died away and we watched the guys in silence for a while, then Mike said, "They're a good bunch, actually. Look at them. Out there, washing that car at one in the morning. And before this, we could hardly get them to wash anything."

The students finished cleaning the car and dried it with a chamois, then pushed it into the shop. Thirty minutes later, they had the hood off with the engine disconnected from its wiring and hoses. I helped them attach the engine to the hoist and we carefully lifted it out of the car, then bolted it to the engine stand.

When that was complete, I attempted to intervene. "I think we've done enough for tonight. We should leave it now and pick this up tomorrow afternoon."

"We have to get this thing ready," Rick said.

"We only have a week," Alan noted.

"It's two a.m.," I replied. "You have to be at Mass in a few hours."

"Okay," Ron called over his shoulder, but he and the others were busy moving things aside to make room for the engine stand.

I gave up. "Okay. The first thing you have to do…"

"We know," Frank said, interrupting. "Wash the engine."

They rolled the engine stand, with the engine attached, outside to the same concrete pad where they'd washed the car. David followed. Pete showed him how to use the power washer and a moment later, he was blasting grime from the engine block.

As the sky turned gray in the east, the energy and emotion that had driven the guys all night began to fade. The car was clean. The engine was clean. And both were back in the shop, ready for the detailed work of learning what went wrong and what needed to be repaired. Everyone was exhausted.

"Okay," I said. "Let's take a break."

"Yeah," Pete admitted. "I'm tired."

"You stink, too," Reuben noted. Everyone laughed.

"We all stink," I added. "So, let's take a shower. Get something to eat. And we can start on the engine this afternoon."

"We still have Mass," Frank said.

"You can sleep in the van on the way into town," I suggested.

They trooped up to the house, then David and I went home. After a shower, I fell asleep in a chair by the sofa. An alarm on my watch awakened me in time to join the guys at church.

CHAPTER 23

Even after spending all night at the shop, everyone made it to St. Francis for Mass that morning, though it was difficult for most to stay awake. Several of the guys nodded off during the service and I had to nudge David once or twice to stop him from snoring. Tommy didn't like it, but Father Brennan, the priest, was amused and Mike had to hide his face once to keep from laughing out loud.

When the service concluded, David and I returned to the cottage for lunch and a nap. When I awakened, I phoned Susan to find out why she wanted to talk. She suggested we meet at her house. I took David to the farmhouse where I intended simply to drop him off, but when we arrived the guys were eager to work on the car. I opened the shop and got them started on disassembling the engine, then left to meet Susan.

During the drive to her house, I thought of the possibilities for what she wanted to talk about. All the usual subjects came to mind—she met someone else. She liked me but didn't think the time was right. She needed to concentrate on other things. Or she loved me and, as crazy as it seemed, she thought we should get married. I laughed at the last one. A woman like her, taking a chance on a barely sober alcoholic using a race car as a project to help fellow addicts see themselves in a new way … not much chance of that happening. But I did hope she wanted to see me again.

Susan opened the front door almost as soon as I rang the doorbell. As if she were standing there, watching for me. I couldn't decide if that was a good sign or not, but I greeted her with a smile just the same.

"Come in," she said, and she backed away to let me by.

When I was inside, she closed the door and stepped toward me. Her arms went around my waist, and she leaned forward to kiss me. And just like that, I was feeling much better about whatever was going to happen. We kissed once, then again, and a third time, I think, though the second was long and I might have lost track of the count.

Eventually, she leaned away and smiled. "You didn't know what to expect, did you?"

"No," I said. "I didn't." My arms were still around her and I pulled her close against me. "You were being mysterious about it." She rested her head against my chest. "What did you want to see me about?"

We stood there for a moment, locked in the warmest embrace I'd ever experienced. The kind that envelopes you and surrounds you and you never want it to end. She turned her head to one side. "There was a job in Houston. My sister wanted me to apply for it. Some of her friends thought it would be a perfect fit. So, I applied."

"And you got the job."

I felt her head nod. "Yes," she said. "Last night, when we were at the track, I told you we needed to talk so I could tell you about it."

"It would have been okay if you had," I replied, though it would have been devastating. We had only become close very recently but chasing down fugitives together seemed to bond us rather quickly. At least, I thought so. But it could have had the opposite effect on her.

"I didn't want to distract you with it," she said. "So, I told you we could talk later. But then I watched you with the guys. The way you handled them when things went wrong…." She looked up at me. "I don't know what will happen to us, but I know this. There are many jobs like the one they offered me. And I still have a good job right here. But there aren't many men like you in the world and whether we make it together or not, you're here and I'm not going anywhere until we find out about us."

Monday morning, I arrived at the shop to find the engine disassembled with the parts lying in order on the workta-ble. One look told me a piston had broken and damaged the head. The cylinder was in good shape, and we could replace the piston, but the head needed attention only a qualified machine shop could provide.

"Is there a shop in Alexandria?" Frank asked. "Maybe Mr. Tapia knows of one."

"I'm sure he does," I replied. "But I think getting it fixed and back to us will take too long. I doubt they can have it ready in time for Saturday. And I'm not sure we have the money for it."

"So, what do we do?" Reuben asked.

"Is that it?" Rick chimed in. "We're done. We're out of the championship?"

Gary spoke up. "What about that?" He was pointing to the engine from the pickup that we had used earlier for demonstrations. "Can't we take the heads off of it?"

"Are they the same size?"

"How can we tell?"

"Would the rules allow it?" someone asked.

"The truck engine is a Chevrolet," I said. "So, we're okay with the rules. But I don't know about the size."

"Measure it," Frank said.

We found a tape measure on the worktable and used it to check the external dimensions, then compared that to the engine we'd removed from the car. To my surprise, they were the same. Then I noted the bolt placement and checked that. They seemed to be the same, too, but there still was the internal configuration to consider. The head might fit onto the block but still not work.

With little difficulty, we removed the heads from the second engine and Pete carried them to the parts washer—a metal sink in the corner of the shop that used a cleaning solvent. It was helpful in washing smaller parts we couldn't clean with the power washer.

After the heads were cleaned, we removed the springs and other parts. The springs on the engine from the car were in good shape and seemed to be better than the ones from the truck, so we kept them, along with the rods and lifters, and only used the heads themselves. It was a lot to do, but late on Tuesday, we had the engine assembled and back in the car. After we'd bolted the last piece in place and re-attached the hood, the guys stood around the car staring at it. Finally, I said, "We have to see if it will run."

"We're too scared," Alan replied.

"Yeah," David added. "It might blow up again."

"It might run great, too," Frank offered.

They all laughed, and we pushed the car outside. I turned to Pete. "Get in and let's find out what we have."

He climbed into the driver's seat and flipped the switch. The engine turned over but didn't start. I wondered if we should continue but before I could speak, Pete stuck his head out the window and shouted, "Get the ether."

Reuben brought the can of ether and sprayed a little in the carburetor, and then Pete tried the engine again. This time it started and, after a few sputters, ran smoothly. We checked for leaks in the cooling system and the oil pan, then turned it off and returned it to the shop.

Alan asked, "What's next?"

"We wait for Saturday," I replied.

As things turned out, the alternate way we chose drivers worked out even, with everyone having an equal number of turns at the steering wheel except David. I brought this to everyone's attention on Saturday afternoon, as we loaded the car onto the trailer for the trip to the track. "We can either continue with the rotation," I said. "Or choose a driver a different way for this race."

Someone suggested David should drive, but he waved them off. "Not me," he said. "Not tonight. This is the last race. We need someone better than me."

"Pete and Frank are the best," Rick said.

Gary agreed. "Y'all flip for it."

That seemed to satisfy everyone, and I handed Pete a quarter. He tossed it into the air. He called heads and won the toss, but he seemed hesitant. "We need our best driver," he said. "Not one chosen by a toss of a coin."

"Who's do you think is the best?" I asked.

"Frank," he replied.

Frank shook his head. "I don't think I'm the—"

"Yeah, you are," Pete insisted. "You're a natural at this."

"Are you sure?"

"Yeah," Pete said. "I really am."

Selflessness is a difficult trait to acquire. Most of us want to grab all the attention we can get for ourselves. When I first arrived at the farm, Pete seemed like a master at self-aggrandizement. Putting that aside for the benefit of others was a big step for him. Everyone in the group noticed.

Susan was waiting for us when we arrived at the track. She stood with me while the guys unloaded the car. "Did you get it fixed?" she asked.

"It runs," I said. "I reckon we'll find out in a few minutes if it'll last the night."

She put her arm in mine. "You're different from when I first saw you."

"Well," I said. "A lot has happened since then."

"It's more than that," she countered. "I know you got the car as a project for the guys, but it has changed everyone. Including you and David and everyone at the farm."

Frank ran the fastest lap in our class and qualified the car in first place. While he waited for the race to start, he remained in the car. I came to the window on the driver's side. "You looked good out there."

"Thanks," he replied.

"How did it feel?"

"Like every other time."

"It sounded like every other time, too," I said. "But I don't know how long that engine will last. So don't push it. We can't win if we don't finish." Other than Susan, no one had mentioned the engine or its condition. I thought Frank ought to consider it.

"We can't win if we finish last either," he noted.

"You only need to finish in sixth place to win the championship."

He looked over at me. "It would be kind of tough not to race everyone."

I felt embarrassed for even suggesting he do less than his best. Most of the guys in the program had been settling for the easy way all their lives, which is how they got into trouble. Having grown passed that, I couldn't really argue that he ought to go back to it now. I gripped his forearm. "Get us a win," I said.

Frank nodded. "See you at the checkered flag."

The race began as usual, with the slower cars in front. But like us, those drivers had driven all summer and improved their ability, too. That night, everyone wanted to win, and they drove more aggressively than before.

As a result, there were three wrecks that produced caution periods, reducing the number of laps for competitive racing. Fewer racing laps limited Frank's ability to come from the back of the field as quickly as he had in previous events. After what proved to be the final caution period, he was in tenth place, four places behind where he needed to be to give our car the championship.

Rick stood next to me. "Think he can do it?"

"He's got a chance," I said. "But he'll have to—"

"Ha!" Pete laughed, interrupting us. "Frank could beat these guys with a tricycle."

I grinned. "He'd probably find a way."

"He'll be in front when they get to the last lap," Pete said confidently. "Just wait. You'll see."

Two laps later, Frank had the car in eighth place. And three laps after that, he was in third. He could have driven the race to the end right there, finished third, and secured the season championship with points to spare. Some would have called it the smart strategy, but that wasn't the way Frank approached things.

One lap after reaching third place, the car ahead of Frank drove too fast into the curve. The extra speed caused the car to slide up the track higher than normal. Frank, traveling slightly slower but with more grip, steered our car lower on the track and came alongside the other car. They were side-by-side on backstretch but at the next turn, Frank completed the pass and moved into second place. There was only one car between him and first place, but only one lap remaining in the race.

On the front stretch, Frank drew even with the first-place car, and they went side-by-side into the curve. In truth, they were only going about seventy miles per hour, but that night it seemed like we were racing at a superspeedway. Everyone in the stands seemed to think so, too. They were standing and cheering as the two cars ran the final lap side-by-side, engines whining, dirt flying in the air, neither driver backing down.

As they came out of the last turn, and started toward the checkered flag, Frank was on the inside. Normally, the car on the outside carried more momentum through the turn and often accelerated quicker onto the straightaway, but this time, the right side of our car didn't slide as much as usual. The tires gripped the surface, getting what older drivers called "a good bite" against the dirt. That extra grip translated into faster acceleration and propelled our car out of the turn like it was shot from a cannon. When the two cars crossed the finish line, Frank was a fender-length in front.

In the infield, the guys screamed and hollered and laughed and hugged each other, dancing around like they didn't really know what to do but had to do something. I took a seat on the trailer, bowed my head to hide my face, and cried.

Susan sat beside me. "He won," she said.

"Yeah," I replied, unable to look at her.

She leaned closer. "You did a good thing for them."

"They did a good thing for me."

"Yes," she said. "They did."

We sat there a moment, neither saying a word, then she took my hand. "Come on. Let's have a look at that championship trophy."

The car was parked at the flag stand. Frank was out of it and holding the checkered flag. The trophy sat on the hood of the car. We all gathered on the opposite side, with the trophy in front, and posed for a photo.

We were standing there with the crowd cheering and Frank holding the checkered flag, but in my mind a thousand different scenes flashed before me. That day in the dorm when Julia called. Telling our parents that she was pregnant. The day David was born. The day Julia took him from the apartment and left. Living on the street. Pump getting shot. Me drunk out of my mind. And Father Deasy rescuing me. No one would have chosen that kind of life. No one could have even imagined it. But despite the misery, and anguish, and guilt, I wouldn't have traded it for anything.

It's odd how that happens. Given a choice that morning when I was sitting at the window in my dorm room, I would have picked a more mundane future for myself. Predictable. Safe. Secure. And I would never have wanted Julia to die or David to have the childhood he experienced. But we don't get a do-over in life and that night at the track with the guys, and David, and Susan, I didn't want one.

FICTION BY JOE HILLEY

THE MIKE CONNOLLY MYSTERY SERIES:

Sober Justice

Double Take

Night Rain

Electric Beach

The Deposition

Sunset Motel

GENERAL FICTION:

What the Red Moon Knows

The Art Dealer's Wife

Kipling Park

SHORT STORY COLLECTIONS:

The Legend of Dell Briggers

Other People, Other Places

For more information, visit Joe's website at: joehilley.com